A wizard is only as good as his spells.

This statement is only made by people who have never been wizards themselves.

Those of us who have chosen to pursue a sorcerous career know that a knowledge of spells is only one small facet of a successful magician. Equally important are a quick wit, a soothing tongue, and, perhaps most important, a thorough knowledge of back alleys, underground passageways, and particularly dense patches of forest . . . for those times when the spell you knew so well doesn't quite work after all.

—from THE TEACHINGS OF EBENEZUM,
Volume I

"*A Malady of Magicks* is a slapstick romp worthy of Laurel & Hardy . . . but I warn you not to read it late at night—the neighbours will call the cops when you laugh down the walls!"

—Marvin Kaye, author of
The Incredible Umbrella

D1341083

A Malady of Magicks

Craig Shaw Gardner

HEADLINE

This first one
is for my mother and father
without whom . . .

Chapter Two originally appeared 'in substantially different form' as 'A Drama of Dragons' in Scott Card's *Dragons of Light* (Ace), copyright © 1980 by Craig Shaw Gardner. Chapters Three and Four appeared, more or less, as 'A Dealing with Demons' in Lin Carter's *Flashing Swords!* #5 (Dell), copyright © 1981 by Craig Shaw Gardner. Chapter Five appeared as 'A Gathering of Ghosts' in Marvin Kaye's *Ghosts* (Doubleday & Co), copyright © 1981 by Craig Shaw Gardner.

First published in Great Britain in 1988
by HEADLINE BOOK PUBLISHING PLC

ISBN 0 7472 3136 2

Printed and bound in Great Britain by
Collins, Glasgow

HEADLINE BOOK PUBLISHING PLC
Headline House
79 Great Titchfield Street
London W1P 7FN

ONE

" 'A wizard is only as good as his spells,' people will often say. It is telling, however, that this statement is only made by people who have never been wizards themselves.

Those of us who have chosen to pursue a sorcerous career know that a knowledge of spells is only one small facet of the successful magician. Equally vital are a quick wit, a soothing tongue, and, perhaps most important, a thorough knowledge of back alleys, underground passageways, and particularly dense patches of forest, for those times when the spell you knew so well doesn't quite work after all."

—THE TEACHINGS OF EBENEZUM, Volume I

The day was quietly beautiful, perhaps too much so. For the first time in a week, I allowed myself to forget my problems and think only of Alea. Alea! My afternoon beauty. I had only learned her name on the last day we were together, before she went on

1

to, as she called them, "better things." But as surely as she had left me, I knew that we might be reunited. In Vushta, anything might happen.

The wizard sneezed.

I woke from my reverie, instantly alert. My master, the wizard Ebenezum, greatest mage in all the Western Kingdoms, had sneezed. It could only mean one thing.

There was sorcery in the air!

Ebenezum waved for me to follow him, his stately and ornate wizard's robes flapping as he ran. We headed immediately for a nearby copse of trees.

A hoarse scream erupted from the bushes across the clearing.

"Death to the wizard!"

The spear embedded itself in the tree some three feet above my head. Half a dozen warriors ran screaming from the undergrowth, blood cries on their lips. They had painted themselves with dark pigments for a particularly fierce appearance, and they carried great swords as long as their arms.

The spear seemed to have a few primitive charms painted on it. Oh, so that was all it was. Just another assassination attempt. In a way, I was disappointed. For a moment, I had thought it might be something serious.

So it began again. By this time, I must admit these assassination things had grown quite tiresome. All thoughts of my afternoon beauty had fled from my mind. As boringly regular as these attacks had become, it would still not do to become too lax in our response.

I looked to my master. The wizard Ebenezum, one of the most learned men upon this huge continent we now traversed, nodded briskly and held his nose.

I placed my hands in the basic third conjuring position. Taking a deep breath, I stepped from concealment.

"Halt, villains!" I cried.

The warriors did nothing to acknowledge my warning, instead bounding across the field toward me with redoubled fury. Their leader's tangled blond hair bounced as he ran, a mobile bird's nest above his brow. He hurled another spear, almost tripping with the effort. His aim was not very good.

I quickly wove a magic pattern with my hands. During the last few days of our headlong flight, Ebenezum had taken what few rest periods we could manage to teach me some basic sign magic. It was all quite simple, really. After you had mastered a few easy gestures, earth, air, fire, and water were yours to command.

Still, I didn't want to try anything too difficult for my first solo endeavor. Another spear whistled through the air, almost impaling the leader of the warrior band from the rear. The leader yelped and stopped his headlong charge. He was close enough that I could see the anger in his pale blue eyes.

Infuriated, he spun to lecture his men on appropriate spear-throwing technique. Ebenezum waved from the trees for me to get on with it. It would be a simple spell, then. I decided I would move the earth with my magic and create a yawning pit in which our pursuers would be trapped. I began making the proper movements with my elbows and left leg, at the same time whistling the first four bars of "The Happy Woodcutter's Song."

The warriors screamed as one and ran toward me with even greater speed. I hurried my spell as well, hopping once, skipping twice, scratching my head, and whistling those four bars again.

The sky suddenly grew dark. My magic was working! I pulled my left ear repeatedly, blowing my nose
in rhythmic bursts.

A great mass of orange dropped from the heavens.

I paused in my gyrations. What had I done? A
layer of orange and yellow covered the field and the
warriors. And the layer was moving.

It took me a moment to discern the layer's true
nature. Butterflies! Somehow, I had conjured millions of them. They flew wildly about the field, doing
their best to get away from the warriors. The warriors, in turn, sputtered and choked and waved their
arms feverishly about, doing their best to get away
from the butterflies.

I had made a mistake somewhere in my spell; that
much was obvious. Luckily, the resulting butterfly
multitude was enough of a diversion to give me time
to correct my error. I reviewed my movements. I had
spent hours perfecting my elbow flaps. The hop, the
skips, the scratch, everything seemed in its place.
Unless I was supposed to lift my right leg rather than
my left?

Of course! How stupid of me! I immediately set
out to repeat the spell and correct my mistake.

The warriors seemed to have won free of the butterflies at last. Breathing heavily, some leaning on
their swords, they gave a ragged yell and staggered
forward. I finished my humming and started to blow
my nose.

The sky grew dark again. The warriors paused in
their hesitant charge and looked aloft with some
trepidation.

This time it rained fish. Dead fish.

The warriors left with what speed they could

muster, slipping and sliding through a field now covered with crushed butterflies and thousands of dead haddock. I decided it was time for us to leave as well. From the smell now rising from the field, the haddock had been dead for quite some time.

"Excellent, apprentice!" My master emerged from his place of concealment among the trees. He still held his nose. "And I had not yet taught you the raining creatures spell. You show a real talent for improvisation. Though how you managed a rain of butterflies and dead fish is beyond me." He shook his head and chuckled to himself. "One could almost imagine you were whistling 'The Happy Woodcutter's Song.'"

We both laughed at the foolishness of that thought and rapidly left the area. I decided I needed to hone my sorcerous skills just a bit before our next encounter, which probably wouldn't be all that long from now. King Urfoo simply wouldn't give up.

A bloodcurdling scream came from far overhead. I looked up in the trees to see a figure, dressed all in green, plummeting in our general direction. The wizard and I watched the man fall some ten feet in front of us, knocking himself unconscious in the process.

Ebenezum and I stepped gingerly around the fallen assassin. Surely another of King Urfoo's minions, incredibly bloodthirsty, and incredibly inept. Urfoo, it seemed, had offered a reward for our death or capture. That alone was enough to attract certain mercenaries. But Urfoo was the cheapest of cheap tyrants, keeping his purse strings tied in a double knot and giving a whole new meaning to the phrase "tight-fisted." The reward for our demise was not all that large, and none of it was payable in advance.

Certain mercenaries, by and large, lost interest when they became familiar with the terms. This left only the foolish, the desperate, and the desperately foolish to pursue us. Which they did. In droves.

I looked down at my worn shoes and torn tunic, aware of every noise in the forest around me, careful of every movement I might see out of the corner of my eye. Who would have thought that I, a poor farm boy from the Western Kingdoms, would find himself in circumstances such as these? What would I have done, on that day when I was first apprenticed to Ebenezum, had I known I would leave the peace and security of a small, rural village, destined to wander through strange kingdoms and stranger adventures? Who would think that I might one day even be forced to visit Vushta, the city of a thousand forbidden delights, and somehow have the courage to face every single one?

I looked to my master, the great wizard Ebenezum, boldly marching by my side, his fine tunic, tastefully inlaid with silver moons and stars, now slightly soiled; his long white hair and beard a tad matted about the edges; his aristocratic nose the merest bit stuffed from his affliction. Who would have thought, on that summer's day a few months ago, that we would come to this?

"Wuntvor!" my master called.

I considered making a hasty retreat.

"No, no, Wuntvor. Come here, please!" Ebenezum smiled and waved. It must be worse than I thought.

I had only been apprenticed to the wizard for a few weeks then and, frankly, didn't care much for the job. My new master hardly spoke to me at all and certainly made no attempt to explain all the strange things going on around me. That is, until he became angry with me for something I'd done. Then there seemed to be no end to his wizardly rage.

And now the gruff wizard was smiling. And waving. And calling my name. I didn't like this situation at all. Why had I become a wizard's apprentice in the first place?

Then I remembered that I had a reason now. A very special reason. Just that morning I had been in the forest, some distance from the house, collecting firewood for use in the magician's never-ending assortment of spells. I had looked up from my gathering, and she had been standing there!

"You seem to have lost your firewood." Her voice was lower than I expected from so slender a girl, and huskier as well. She formed each word with a pair of perfect lips. I looked down to the pile of wood at my feet. One look at her long-haired splendor, and my arms had gone limp.

"Yes, I have," was all I could think to say.

"Whom do you gather it for?" she asked.

I nodded toward the cabin, just visible through the trees. "The wizard."

"The wizard?" Her lips parted to show a smile that would make the angels sing. "You work for a wizard?"

I nodded. "I am his apprentice."

Her finely etched brows rose in pleased surprise. "An apprentice? I must say, that's much more interesting than most of what goes on hereabouts." She flashed me a final smile.

"We will have to see each other again," she whispered, and was gone.

I thought on that at the door to the master's study. She wanted to see me again. And simply because I was a magician's apprentice!

Ebenezum called my name once more.

My afternoon beauty! It was a good thing to be magician's apprentice, after all! I took a deep breath and entered the magician's study.

"Over here, Wuntvor." My master pulled forward a stool for me. "I will show you how to construct a spell." That smile showed again, curling through the space between his mustache and his long white beard. "A very special spell."

The wizard's robes swirled as he turned. The stars and the moons embroidered on the cloth danced in the candlelight. Ebenezum pushed his cap to a jaunty angle and walked over to an immense oak table that was almost entirely covered by a huge, open book.

"Most spells," the wizard began, "are quite mundane. Plying one's trade in a rural clime such as this, any wizard, even one as experienced as myself, finds most of his or her time occupied with increased crop yield spells, and removing curses from sheep and the like. Now, why anyone would want to curse a sheep is beyond my comprehension"—the wizard paused to glance in his book—"but a job is a job and a fee is a fee. And that, Wuntvor, is the first law of wizardry."

Ebenezum picked up one of two long white candles that sat at either side of the table. He placed it in the only clear spot on the study's floor. The candlelight illuminated a star, sketched in the dirt.

"The second law is to always stay one step ahead of the competition," he continued. "As I was saying, you'll soon tire of crop and curse spells. As far as I'm concerned, you're not a full-fledged wizard until they really bore you. But in your spare time—ah, Wuntvor, that's when you'll find the opportunity for your wizardry to shine!''

I watched my master with mute fascination. He moved quickly about his study, turning here, kneeling there, fetching a book or a gnarled root or some strange, sorcerous device. I could half imagine his wanderings set to music, like some mysterious dance to herald the coming magic. The whole thing was something of a revelation; like cracking open a piece of slate to find the speckled blue of a robin's egg.

"And now we begin." My master's eyes seemed to sparkle in the reflected candle flame. "When this spell is finished, I shall know the exact position, disposition, and probably future direction of every tax collector in the realm!"

So this is what my master did in his spare time. I imagined there was some greater scheme to the spell that he had just described that I did not yet see, but I judged it a bad time to ask for explanations.

My master pulled back his sleeves with a flourish. "Now we begin!"

He hesitated at the edge of the markings. "But my enthusiasm carries me away. Wuntvor, something seems to be on your mind. Did you have a question?"

So I told him about the bucket.

I mean well, but my hands do not always do exactly what my mind intends. Growing pains, my mother always called them. On perhaps in this case, the thought of the girl I had encountered in the woods. At any rate, I dropped the bucket, without the rope, into the well.

What could I do? I stared dumbly at the length of rope I had wanted to tie around the handle. I should never have set the bucket on the well's edge. I looked down into the well but couldn't see a thing in the gloom. I kicked the side of the well. If only, somehow, the rope could magically tie itself to the bucket, everything would be fine.

And then I realized that the rope *could* magically tie itself to the bucket. So I ran to the wizard's study to ask for help. That is, if he wasn't too busy.

"Oh, I think I can fit it in," the wizard replied. "You do sometimes have a problem with your hands, Wuntvor. Not to mention your feet, your height, and a few other things. Still, with luck, you should grow out of it."

Ebenezum pulled at his beard. "There's a lesson to be learned here, Wuntvor. If you intend to be a wizard, you must consider your every action carefully. Every action, from the smallest to the largest, might somehow affect your performance of magic, and thus your fortunes and possibly your life. Now let's fetch the bucket and get on with things."

I stood to lead my master to the well. But instead of walking to the door, the wizard took a half step back and raised his arms. His low voice murmured a dozen syllables. Something bumped against my knee. It was the bucket.

"Now—" the wizard began just before he yelled in surprise. "What the—" He leapt forward and turned to face whatever had upset him.

It was smoke, or so it seemed at first; a particularly vile-smelling cloud of bluish gray that hung over the star drawn in the dirt. It swirled about furiously, growing until it almost looked like a human shape.

The wizard pointed to the ground. There was a smudge across the markings on the floor where the mystically propelled bucket had passed.

"The pentagram!" Ebenezum cried. "I've broken the pentagram!"

He grabbed a small knife from the table and knelt by the side of the star. He placed the knife against what remained of the line and used it to redraw the markings up to the point where he was stopped by a huge blue foot. The foot was attached to an even larger body; a body made of almost nothing but spikes, talons, and horns.

"A demon!" I cried.

The thing opened its mouth. Its voice was as deep as an earthquake. "Sound the charge and ring the bells," it said. "You have freed me from the Nether-hells!"

Ebenezum's lips curled behind his mustache. "Even worse, Wuntvor. 'Tis a rhyming demon!"

The giant blue thing took a step toward the candle-light. As it approached the illumination, I could make out what in charity might be described as facial features: a knife slash for a mouth, above that a pair of hairy nostrils, and a couple of eyes too small and evil to even be called beady.

The thing spoke again:

"Alas, you humans are out of luck,
  For now you face the demon Guxx!"

"Luck and Guxx?" Ebenezum's face became even more distraught. "That's not even a proper rhyme!"

Guxx the demon displayed its dark and pointed claws. "I'm somewhat new at the poetry game. But you'll soon be dead all the same!"

Ebenezum glanced at me. "See what I mean? The meter's all wrong." The wizard pulled at his beard. "Or maybe it's the creature's delivery."

"You try to confuse me with your words!" the demon cried. "But Guxx will shorten you by a third!"

The demon's claws shot out with lightning speed, straight for the wizard's neck. But Ebenezum was every bit as fast as the creature, and the claws only grazed his magician's cap.

"You're getting too complex," the wizard remarked as he pulled back his sleeves. Ebenezum liked both arms free to the elbows for maximum conjuring. "You'd be better to stick to simpler rhymes."

The demon paused in its attack, a deep rumble in its throat. "Perhaps," it said, and coughed into one of its enormous palms.

"Guxx Unfufadoo is my name,
    And killing wizards is my game!"

Ebenezum's hands made a complex series of movements in the air as he spoke half a dozen syllables that I didn't understand. The demon roared. It was surrounded by a silver cage.

"You think to stop me with your silver!" Guxx screamed. "But I'll break free and eat your—" It paused. "No. That doesn't work. What rhymes with silver?"

"Orange," the wizard suggested.

"I'll teach you this demon to mock! A few more rhymes, and I'll break this lock!" The creature stared at its cage. The bars shook without it even touching them.

"This demon could be a bit of a problem," Ebenezum said. "Come, Wuntvor. I will teach you a quick lesson in banishment."

"Guxx will win, this demon knows!
For with every rhyme my power grows!"

"Yes, yes. Bear with us for a moment, won't you? That's a good demon." Ebenezum glanced over one of the dozens of bookshelves that cluttered the room. "Ah. The very tome."

He extracted a thin brown volume from the upper shelf. *312 More Easy Banishment Spells* was stamped in gold on the cover.

"Now, as I remember it . . ." Ebenezum paused as he leafed through the book. "In a case such as this, Wuntvor, it is important that you find just the right spell. Saves messy cleanup afterward. Ah, here's the very one!"

"Don't talk of spells, don't talk of mess, for seconds from now Guxx will bring your death!" the hideous creature cried.

"If your power grows with that rhyme," Ebenezum remarked, "there is no justice in the cosmos." The wizard cleared his throat. "At least no poetic justice."

"You make awful jokes at my expense,
But from Guxx's claws you'll have no defense!"

With that, the demon's arms burst through the sides of the silver cage.

"Back, Wuntvor!" the wizard cried.

The demon was on top of Ebenezum. It had moved

faster than my eyes could follow it. Razor claws whistled as they descended on the wizard.

My master was in dire peril. I had to do something!

I jumped for the thing's back. Guxx shrugged, and I was tossed aside.

Ebenezum shouted something, and the demon was thrown across the room. The wizard staggered to his feet. His right sleeve was torn. The arm beneath was bright with blood.

" 'Twill soon be finished, come now, make
    haste!
A wizard's blood is to my taste!"

The demon smiled.

Ebenezum grabbed a box from the shelf behind him. He tossed the contents at the approaching Guxx. Yellow powder filled the air. And the world slowed down.

Guxx was no longer a blur. You could see the demon's every movement now as its heavily muscled form strained against whatever the yellow powder had done. I could feel the effects as well. Sitting on the edge of the conflict, it took an eternity to turn my head or blink my eyes.

Ebenezum still seemed to be moving at normal speed. His voice cried a tuneless song, and his hands wove swirling patterns upward, ever upward, like two birds seeking the sun.

The demon was moving faster. Its slow progress had become a walk.

Small points of light appeared above the wizard's hands; dancing light that described fantastic shapes as it circled the upper reaches of the room.

The demon flicked aside the great oak table. Its

movement was as fast as any man's.

The wizard snapped his fingers, and light flew at the demon's head. The demon cried in pain, its claws splayed out at the open air.

"Death is coming, wizard!" it screamed. Then, a moment later, as if an afterthought: "I'll cut out your gizzard!"

"Gizzard?" The wizard reached for something in his sleeve. "Well, I suppose it's more appropriate than blizzard."

The demon leapt for the mage. And Ebenezum had pulled a short sword from the folds of his cloak.

So it would come to hand-to-hand combat. But the demon was clearly stronger than the wizard. There had to be some way I could help! I stood and almost tripped over the bucket. If only I had a sword as well!

Dagger met claws. And the claws were sheared in half.

Guxx screamed with a rage that shook the floor beneath me. The creature darted away from the wizard and swatted the air with its blunted talons. Holding the dagger before him, Ebenezum stepped toward the demon.

What was my master doing? He had virtually walked into the demon's arms. Guxx's still-taloned hand was behind the wizard now, aimed for the back of Ebenezum's head.

I had to do something. So I threw the bucket.

Bucket met talons, and the claws sliced through the wood as if it were paper. But Ebenezum whirled about as the bucket split. Dagger met claws again, and Guxx had lost all its weapons. Or so I thought before the demon opened its mouth. There were two rows of sharpened spikes where the creature's teeth should be.

It was a frightening sight. The mage backed away from the fiend's gaping maw, but Guxx was faster. The demon's deadly incisors caught Ebenezum's beard.

The wizard tried to call out a spell, but his words dribbled away as he choked in the demon's foul breath, so close to his own. Although the demon's mouth was largely occupied by beard, the corners of the fiend's lips appeared to smile. But only for an instant, for Guxx, too, must have realized the flaw in its demonic plan.

By capturing the wizard's beard, and contaminating the mage's air with its own exhalations, Guxx had put an end to Ebenezum's magicks. But since the demon's own mouth was filled with wizard hair, Guxx could not utter that final, devastating poem that would make it a victor of this sorcerous contest. The demon furrowed its immense brow, causing its incredibly tiny eyes to appear even tinier.

The combatants had reached a stalemate. But Ebenezum could not hold his own for long. Guxx's demon breath prevented not only the wizard's speech, but cut off the mage's supply of wholesome air. Ebenezum was rapidly turning a color not unlike a robin's egg, or certain pebbles I have found at river bottom. It was not a hue that particularly suited him.

If I did not act quickly, Guxx would win by default.

I looked about for a weapon, but all I could see were the broken bucket and a half dozen sheared claws. The claws! What better way to defeat a demon?

I grabbed a pair of the deadly daggers, one for each hand. The claws were the length of my longest finger.

"Take that, fiend!" I cried, plunging them toward the demon's rib cage.

The claws bounced from Guxx's stonelike skin. The demon made a deep sound, like rocks dropped down a well. After a second's hesitation, I realized it was laughter.

So it would be harder than I thought. But I must save my master! I struck again, with redoubled force.

The claws made a scratching sound this time as they slid across the demon's hide. Guxx laughed even louder. He couldn't control the laughter; tears ran out of his pinpoint eyes. Ebenezum pulled back at the fiend's mirth and managed to free a small portion of his beard.

I threw myself at the demon, both claws running up and down its fearsome rib cage. Guxx reared back its head and roared helplessly.

Ebenezum was free!

The mage shouted something, and the demon seemed to grow smaller. It grabbed at the wizard's robes with the remains of its claws. Ebenezum made a series of passes in the air, and Guxx once again turned to blue smoke, which was sucked in turn back into the pentacle from which it came.

The wizard half sat, half fell into the dirt. His beard was matted and ragged. The demon had torn fully half of it away.

"Open the windows, Wuntvor," he managed after a minute. "We need to clean the air."

I did as I was told, and the last bits of the blue cloud vanished with the breeze. That's when the wizard began to sneeze.

It was a sneezing fit, really. My master couldn't stop. He lay on the ground, sneezing over and over again. I remembered his remarks about clearing the air. Even with the windows open, the atmosphere in the study was far from wholesome. I thought I should get him outside, in the open. Which, with some difficulty, I managed to do.

His fit ended almost as soon as we were out in daylight, but it took him a moment to catch his breath.

"Never have I had such a fight," he whispered. "I was worried there for a time, Wuntvor." He shook his head. "No matter. It is over now."

Unfortunately, Ebenezum was wrong. It was only just beginning.

TWO

"Reasoned decision is important, and there comes a time in every wizard's life when he must decide what goal he should pursue to give true meaning to his life. Should it be money, or travel, or fame? And what of leisure and the love of women? I myself have studied many of these goals for a number of years, examining their every facet in some detail, so that, when the time comes to make that fateful decision of which I spoke, it will be reasoned in the extreme."

—THE TEACHINGS OF EBENEZUM, Volume XXXI

I could no longer bring myself to gather firewood. My world had ended. She hadn't come.

I sat for far too long in the sunlit glade where we always met. Perhaps she didn't realize it was noon, she had somehow been delayed, her cool blue eyes and fair blond hair, the way her slim young body moved, the way she laughed, how it felt when she touched me. Surely she was on her way.

Oh, there had been other women: Aneath, the farmer's daughter; what a child I had been then! And Grisla, daughter of the village tinsmith; nothing more than a passing infatuation. Only now did I know the true meaning of love!

But I didn't even know her name! Only her interest in me—a magician's apprentice. She once called magicians the closest thing to play actors she knew in this backwater place. She said she had always admired the stage. And then she laughed, and we kissed, and—

A cold breeze sprang up behind me. A reminder of winter, due all too soon. I gathered what logs and branches I could find and trudged back to my master's cottage.

In the distance I heard a sneeze. So my master was studying his tomes again. Or attempting to study them. Spring had turned to summer, and summer threatened to give way to autumn any day, and still his malady lingered. Ebenezum studied his every waking hour, searching for a cure, but all things magical still brought an immediate nasal reaction. In the meantime, he had handled a handful of commissions, working more with his wits than his spells, so that we might continue to eat. And just this morning, he had mentioned something about a new discovery he had made; a magic spell so quick and powerful that his nose would not have time to react.

Yet still he sneezed. Had his latest experiment failed as well? Why else would he sneeze?

Unless there was something sorcerous in the air.

Perhaps there was another reason besides my mood that the world was so dark around me, another reason that she hadn't met me as we'd planned. The bushes moved on my right. Something very large flew across the sun.

I managed the front door with the firewood still in my arms. I heard the wizard sneeze. Repeatedly. My master stood in the main room, one of his great books spread on the table before him. Smaller books and papers were scattered everywhere, victims of his nasal storm. I hurried to his aid, forgetting, in my haste, the firewood that scattered across the table as I reached for the book. A few miscellaneous pieces fell among the sneezing Ebenezum's robes.

I closed the book and glanced apprehensively at the mage. To my surprise, Ebenezum blew his nose on a gold-inlaid, dark blue sleeve and spoke to me in the calmest of tones.

"Thank you, 'prentice." He delicately removed a branch from his lap and laid it on the table. "If you would dispose of this in a more appropriate place?"

He sighed deep in his throat. "I'm afraid that my affliction is far worse than I imagined. I may even have to call on outside assistance for my cure."

I hastened to retrieve the firewood. "Outside assistance?" I inquired discreetly.

"We must seek out another magician as great as I," Ebenezum said, his every word heavy with import. "Though to do that, we might have to travel as far as the great city of Vushta."

"Vushta?" I replied. "With its pleasure gardens and forbidden palaces? The city of unknown sins that could doom a man for life? That Vushta?" All at once, I felt the lethargy lift from my shoulders. I quickly deposited the wood by the fireplace.

"That Vushta." Ebenezum nodded. "With one problem. We have not the funds for traveling, and no prospects for gaining same."

As if responding to our plight, a great gust of wind blew against the side of the cottage. The door burst open with a swirl of dirt and leaves, and a short man wearing tattered clothes, face besmirched with grime, staggered in and slammed the door behind him.

"Flee! Flee!" the newcomer cried in a quavering voice. "Dragons! Dragons!" With that, his eyes rolled up in his head and he collapsed on the floor.

"I have found, however," Ebenezum said as he stroked his long white beard, "in my long career as a magician, Wuntvor, if you wait around long enough, something is bound to turn up."

With some water on the head and some wine down the gullet, we managed to revive the newcomer.

"Flee!" he sputtered as he caught his breath. He glanced about wildly, his pale eyes darting from my master to me to floor to ceiling. He seemed close to my master in age, but there the similarity ceased. Rather than my master's mane of fine white hair, the newcomer was balding, his hair matted and stringy. Instead of the wizard's masterful face, which could convey calm serenity or cosmic anger with the flick of an eyebrow, the other's face was evasive; small nose and chin, a very wrinkled brow, and those eyes, darting blue in his dark, mud-spattered face.

"Now, now, good sir," Ebenezum replied in his most reasonable voice, often used to charm young ladies and calm bill collectors. "Why the hurry? You mentioned dragons?"

"Dragons!" The man stood somewhat shakily. "Well, at least dragon! One of them has captured Gurnish Keep!"

"Gurnish Keep?" I queried.

"You've seen it," Ebenezum murmured, his cold gray eyes still on our guest. " 'Tis a small castle on yonder hill at the far side of the woods." Ebenezum snorted in his beard. "Castle? 'Tis really more of a stone hut, but it's the home of our neighbor, the Duke of Gurnish. It's a very small dukedom. For that matter, he's a very small duke."

Our visitor was, if anything, even more agitated than before. "I didn't run all the way through Gurnish Forest to hear a discussion of the neighborhood. We must flee!"

"Gurnish Forest?" I inquired.

"The trees right behind the hut," my master replied. "Surely the duke's idea. Everyone else knows the area as Wizard's Woods."

"What do you mean, Wizard's Woods?" the newcomer snapped. "This area is Gurnish Forest. Officially. As Gurnish Keep is an official castle!"

"'Tis only a matter of opinion," Ebenezum replied, a smile that could charm both barbarians and maiden aunts once again upon his face. "Haven't we met somewhere before?"

"Possibly." The newcomer, who was somewhat shorter than my master's imposing frame, shifted uneasily under the wizard's gaze. "But shouldn't we flee? Dragons, you know."

"Come now, man. I wouldn't be a full-fledged wizard if I hadn't dealt with a dragon or two." Ebenezum looked even more closely at the newcomer than he had before. "Say, aren't you the Duke of Gurnish?"

"Me?" the smaller man said. His eyes shifted from my master to me and back again. "Well—uh . . ." He coughed. "I suppose I am."

"Well, why didn't you say so? I haven't seen you

since you stopped trying to tax me." Ebenezum's
smile went to its broadest as he signaled me to get our
guest a chair. The duke obviously had money.

"Well, this whole situation's a bit awkward," our
honored guest said as he stared at the floor. "I'm
afraid I feel rather undukish."

"Nonsense. A run-in with a dragon can unnerve
anyone. Would you like some more wine? A nice fire
to warm you?"

"No, thank you." The duke lowered his voice even
more than before. "Don't you think it would be better if we fled? I mean, dragons. And I've seen other
things in the forest. Perhaps if your powers were—"
The duke coughed again. "You see, I've heard of
your accident."

Ebenezum bristled a bit at the last reference, but
the smile more or less remained on his face. "Gossip,
good duke. Totally blown out of proportion. We'll
deal with your dragon in no time."

"But the dragon's taken over Gurnish Keep! He's
immense, with bright blue and violet scales, twenty-
five feet from head to tail. His wings scrape the
ceiling of my great hall! And he's invincible. He's
captured my castle and beautiful daughter, and
defeated my retainer!"

Beautiful daughter? My thoughts returned to the
girl of my dreams. Where had she gone? What had
kept her away?

"Only a child!" the duke cried. "No more than
seventeen. Fine blond hair, gorgeous blue eyes, a
lovely, girlish figure. And the dragon will burn her to
a crisp if we don't do his bidding!"

Blond? Blue? Figure?

I had a revelation.

"Come now, man," Ebenezum remarked. "Calm

down. It's common knowledge that dragons tend to be overdramatic. All the beast's really done so far is to overwhelm one retainer. I assume you still had only one retainer?''

She hadn't deserted me! She was only held prisoner! All the time she and I had spent together, all those long, warm afternoons. That's why she would tell me nothing of herself! A duke's daughter!

The duke glared at my master. "It wouldn't be like that if my subjects paid their taxes!''

A duke's daughter. And I would rescue her! There'd be no need for secrecy then. How magnificent our lives would be!

A fire lit in Ebenezum's eyes. "Perhaps if certain local royalty were not so concerned with extending the borders of their tiny dukedom . . ." The wizard waved his hands and the fire disappeared. "But that's not important. We have a dragon to evict. As I see it, the elements here are quite ordinary. Dragon captures castle and maiden. Very little originality. We should be able to handle it tidily.''

The duke began to object again, but Ebenezum would have none of it. Only one thing affected his nose more than sorcery—money, and the smell of it was obvious in the cottage. My master sent the duke aside while we gathered the paraphernalia together for dragon fighting.

When I had packed everything according to my master's instructions, Ebenezum beckoned me into his library. Once in the room, the wizard climbed a small stepladder and, carefully holding his nose, pulled a slim volume from the uppermost shelf.

"We may have need of this." His voice sounded strangely hollow, most likely the result of thumb and forefinger pressed into his nose. "In my present condition, I can't risk using it. But it should be easy enough for you to master."

He descended the ladder and placed the thin, dark volume in my hands. Embossed in gold on the cover were the words *How to Speak Dragon*.

"But we must be off!" Ebenezum exclaimed, clapping my shoulder. "Mustn't keep a client waiting. You may study that book on our rest stops along the way."

I stuffed the book hurriedly into the paraphernalia-filled pack and shouldered the whole thing, grabbed my walking staff, and followed my master out the door. With my afternoon beauty at the end of my journey, I could manage anything.

My master had already grabbed the duke by the collar and propelled him in the proper direction. I followed at Ebenezum's heels as fast as the heavy pack would allow. The wizard, as usual, carried nothing. As he often explained, it kept his hands free for quick conjuring and his mind free for sorcerous conjecture.

I noticed a bush move, then another. Rustling like the wind pushed through the leaves, except there was no wind. The forest was as still as when I had waited for my secret love. Still, the bushes moved.

Just my imagination, I thought. Like the darkness of the forest. I glanced nervously at the sky, half expecting the sun to disappear again. What was so big that it blotted out the sun?

A dragon?

But my musings were cut short by a man dressed in bright orange who stood in our path. He peered through an odd instrument on the end of a pole.

I glanced at the duke, walking now at my side. He had begun to shiver.

The man in orange looked up as we approached. "Good afternoon," he said, the half frown on his face belying his words. "Could you move a little faster? You're blocking the emperor's highway, you know."

The duke shook violently.

"Highway?" Ebenezum asked, stopping midpath rather than hurrying by the man in orange.

"Yes, the new road that the great and good Emperor Flostock the Third has decreed—"

"Flee!" the duke cried. "Dragons! Dragons! Flee!" He leapt about, waving his hands before the emperor's representative.

"See here!" the orange man snapped. "I'll have none of this. I'm traveling to see the Duke of Gurnish on important business."

The duke stopped hopping. "Duke?" he said, pulling his soiled clothing back into place. "Why, I'm the Duke of Gurnish. What can I help you with, my good man?"

The man in orange frowned even more deeply. "It's about the upkeep of the road. . . ."

"Certainly." The duke glanced back at us. "Perhaps we should go somewhere that we can talk undisturbed."

The duke led the man in orange into the underbrush.

"They deserve each other," Ebenezum muttered. "But to business." He looked at me solemnly. "A bit about dragons. Dragons are one of the magical subspecies. They exist largely between worlds, partly on Earth and partly in the Netherhells, and never truly belong to either. There are other magical subspecies—"

Ebenezum's lecture was interrupted by a commotion in the underbrush. Large arms with a thick growth of grayish-brown hair rose and fell above the bushes, accompanied by human screams.

"Another subspecies is the troll," Ebenezum remarked.

I let my pack slide from my back and firmly grasped my staff. They would eat my true love's father! I had never encountered trolls before, but this was as good a time as any to learn.

"Slobber! Slobber!" came from the bushes before us. A rough voice, the sound of a saw biting into hardwood. I assumed it was a troll.

"Wait!" another voice screamed. "You can't do this! I'm a representative of the emperor!"

"Slobber! Slobber!" answered a chorus of rough voices.

"Let's get this over with!" Another voice, high and shaky. The duke?

Although the voices were quite close now, it was getting difficult to distinguish individual words. It just sounded like a large amount of screaming, punctuated by cries of "Slobber!" I lifted my staff over my head and ran forward with a scream of my own.

I broke into a small clearing, which contained four occupants. One was the duke. The other three were among the ugliest creatures I'd seen in my short life. They were squat and covered with irregular tufts of gray-brown fur, that did nothing to hide the rippling muscles of their barrellike arms and legs. Three pairs of very small red eyes turned to regard me. One of them swallowed something that looked a good deal like an orange-clad foot.

The sight of the three hideous creatures completely stopped my forward motion. They studied me in silence.

"Oh, hello," I said, breaking into the sinister quiet. "I must have wandered off the path. Excuse me."

One of the trolls lumbered toward me on its immensely powerful legs. It was time to leave. I turned and bumped into my master, who was in the midst of making a mystic gesture.

"No slobber! No slobber!" the trolls cried, and ran back into the heart of the woods.

I picked myself up and helped the wizard regain his feet as well. Ebenezum sneezed for a full three minutes, the result of his actually employing magic. When he caught his breath at last, he wiped his nose on his robe and regarded me evenly.

"Wuntvor," he said, all too quietly, "what do you mean by dropping all our valuable equipment and running off, just so you can be swallowed by—"

The duke ran between the two of us. "Flee! Flee! Dragons! Trolls! Flee!"

"And you!" my master said, his voice rising at last. "I've had enough of your jumping about, screaming hysterical warnings! Why do you worry? You were surrounded by trolls and they didn't touch you. You lead a charmed life!" He grabbed the duke's shoulder with one hand and mine with the other and propelled us back to the trail.

"Come," he continued. "We will reach Gurnish Keep before nightfall. There, my assistant and I will deal with this dragon, and you, good duke, will pay us handsomely for our efforts." The wizard deposited us on the trail and walked briskly toward the castle before the duke could reply.

"Look!" The duke pulled at my sleeve. There was a break in the trees ahead, affording a clear view of the hill on the wood's far side. There, atop the hill, was Gurnish Keep, a stone building not much larger than Ebenezum's cottage. Smoke poured from the keep's lower windows, and once or twice I thought I saw the yellow-orange flicker of flame.

"Dragon," the duke whispered. I hurriedly reached into my satchel and pulled out *How to Speak Dragon*. The time to start learning was now.

I opened the book at random and scanned the page. Phrases in common speech filled one side. Opposite these were the same phrases in dragon. I started reading from the top:

"Pardon me, but could you please turn your snout?"

"*Sniz mir heeba-heeba szzz.*"

"Pardon me, but your claw is in my leg."

"*Sniz mu sazza grack szzz.*"

"Pardon me, but your barbed tail is waving perilously close . . ."

The whole page was filled with similar phrases. I paused in my reading. It had done nothing to reassure me.

Ebenezum shouted at us from far up the trail. I slammed the book shut and ran to follow, dragging the Duke of Gurnish with me.

We walked through the remaining forest without further difficulty. The woods ended at the edge of a large hill, called Wizard's Knoll or Mount Gurnish, depending upon whom you spoke with. From there, we could get a clear view of the castle. And the smoke. And the flames.

The duke began to jabber again about the dangers ahead but was silenced by a single glance from my master. The wizard's cool gray eyes stared up toward the castle, but somehow beyond it. After a moment, he shook his head and flexed his shoulders beneath his robes. He turned to me.

"Wunt," he said. "More occurs here than meets the eye." He glanced again at the duke, who was nervously dancing on a pile of leaves. "Not just a dragon, but three trolls. That's a great deal of supernatural activity for a place as quiet as Wizard's Woods."

I expected the duke to object to the wizard's choice of names, but he was strangely quiet. I turned to the pile of leaves.

The duke was gone.

"Methinks," Ebenezum continued, "some contact has been made with the Netherhells of late. There is a certain instrument in your pack . . ."

My master went on to describe the instrument and its function. If we set it up at the base of the hill, it would tell us the exact number and variety of creatures from the Netherhells lurking about the district.

I held up the instrument. My master rubbed his nose. "Keep it at a distance. The device carries substantial residual magic."

I put the thing together according to the wizard's instructions and, at his signal, spun the gyroscope that topped it off.

"Now, small points of light will appear." Ebenezum sniffled loudly. "You can tell by the color of—"

He sneezed mightily, again and again. I looked to the device. Should I stop it?

Ebenezum sneezed to end all sneezes, directly at the instrument. The device fell apart.

"By the Netherhells!" Ebenezum exclaimed. "Can

I not perform the simplest of spells?'' He looked at me, and his face seemed very old. "Put away the apparatus, Wunt. We must use the direct approach. Duke?''

I explained that the duke had vanished.

"What now?'' Ebenezum looked back toward the forest. His cold gray eyes went wide. He blew his nose hastily.

"Wunt! Empty the pack!''

"What?'' I asked, startled by the urgency of my master's voice. Then I looked back to the woods and saw it coming. A wall of black, like some impenetrable cloud, roiling across the forest. But this cloud extended from the sky to the forest floor and left complete blackness behind. It sped across the woods like a living curtain that drew its darkness ever closer.

"Someone plays with great forces,'' Ebenezum said. "Forces he doesn't understand. The pack, Wunt!''

I dumped the pack's contents on the ground. Ebenezum rifled through them, tossing various arcane tomes and irreplaceable devices out of his way, until he grasped a small box painted a shiny robin's-egg blue.

The magician sneezed in triumph. He tossed me the box.

"Quick, Wunt!'' he called, blowing his nose. "Take the dust within that box and spread it in a line along the hill!'' He waved at a rocky ridge on the forest edge as he jogged up the hill and began to sneeze again.

I did as my master bid, laying an irregular line of blue powder across the long granite slab. I looked back to the woods. The darkness was very close, engulfing all but the forest's edge.

"Run, Wunt!"

I sprinted up the hill. The wizard cried a few ragged syllables and followed. He tripped as he reached the hilltop and fell into an uncontrollable sneezing fit.

I turned back to look at the approaching blackness. The darkly tumbling wall covered all the forest now, and tendrils of the stuff reached out toward the hill like so many grasping hands. But the fog's forward motion had stopped just short of the ragged blue line.

There was a breeze at my back. I turned to see Ebenezum, still sneezing but somehow standing. One arm covered his nose, the other reached for the sky. His free hand moved, and the breeze grew to a wind and then a gale, rushing down the hill and pushing the dark back to wherever it had come.

After a minute the wind died, but what wisps of fog remained in the forest below soon evaporated beneath the bright afternoon sun. My master sat heavily and gasped for breath, as if all the air had escaped from his lungs.

"Lucky," he said after a minute. "Whoever raised the demon fog had a weak will. Otherwise . . ." The magician blew his nose, allowing the rest of the sentence to go unsaid.

A figure moved through the woods beneath us. It was the duke.

"Too exhausted to fight dragon," Ebenezum continued, still breathing far too hard. "You'll have to do it, Wunt."

I swallowed and picked up *How to Speak Dragon* from the hillside where it lay. I turned to look at Gurnish Keep, a scant hundred yards across the hilltop.

Billows of smoke poured from the windows, occasionally accompanied by licks of flame. And now that we stood close, I could hear a low rumble, underlying all the other sounds in the field in which we stood. A rumble that occasionally grew into a roar.

The dragon was going to be everything that I expected.

The duke grabbed at my coat sleeve. "Dragon!" he said. "Last chance to get out!"

"Time to go in there," Ebenezum said. "Look in the book, Wunt. Perhaps we can talk the dragon out of the castle." He shook the quivering duke from his arm. "And if you, good sir, would be quiet for a moment, we could go about saving your home and daughter. Quite honestly, I feel you have no cause for complaint with the luck you've been having. Most people would not have survived the evil spell that recently took over the woods. How you managed to bumble through the powerful forces at work here is beyond . . ." Ebenezum's voice trailed off. He cocked an eyebrow at the duke and stroked his beard in thought.

The rumble from the castle grew louder again. I opened the thin volume I held in my sweating palms; I had to save my secret love.

I flipped frantically from page to page, finally finding a phrase I thought appropriate:

"Pardon me, but might we speak to you?"

In the loudest voice I could manage, I spat out the dragon syllables.

"Snzz grah! Subba Ubba Szzz!"

A great, deep voice reverberated from within the castle. "Speak the common tongue, would you?" it said. "Besides, I'm afraid I don't have a commode."

I closed the book with a sigh of relief. The dragon spoke human!

"Don't trust him!" the duke cried. "Dragons are deceitful!"

Ebenezum nodded his head. "Proceed with caution, Wunt. Someone *is* being deceitful." He turned to the duke. "You!"

"Me?" the Gurnish nobleman replied as he backed in my direction. Ebenezum stalked after him.

They were squabbling again. But I had no time for petty quarrels. I firmly grasped my staff, ready to confront the dragon and my afternoon beauty.

The duke was right behind me now, his courage seemingly returned. "Go forward, wizard!" he cried in a loud voice. "Defeat the dragon! Banish him forever!"

"Oh, not a wizard, too!" cried the voice from within the castle. "First I get cooped up in Gurnish Keep, then I have to capture your beautiful daughter, and now a wizard! How dull! Doesn't anyone have any imagination around here?"

I came to a great oak door. I nudged it with my foot. It opened easily, and I stepped inside to confront the dragon.

It stood on its haunches, regarding me in turn. It was everything the duke had mentioned, and more. Blue and violet scales, twenty-five feet in length, wings that brushed the ceiling. The one oversight in the duke's description appeared to be the large green top hat on the dragon's head.

I saw her a second later.

She stood in front and slightly to one side of the giant reptile. She was as lovely as I'd ever seen her.

"Why, Wuntvor," she said. "What are you doing here?"

I cleared my throat and pounded my staff on the worn stone pavement. "I've come to rescue you."

"Rescue?" She looked up at the dragon. The dragon rumbled. "So Father's gotten to you, too?"

The duke's voice screamed behind me. "I warned you! Now the dragon will burn you all to cinders!"

The dragon snorted good-naturedly and turned to regard the ceiling.

"The game is up, Duke!" Ebenezum called from the doorway, far enough away so that the dragon's magical odor would not provoke another attack. "Your sorcerous schemes are at an end!"

"Yes, Father," my afternoon beauty said. "Don't you think you've gone far enough?" She looked at my master. "Father so much wanted control of the new Trans-Empire Highway, to put toll stations throughout the woods below, that he traded in his best retainer for the services of certain creatures from the Netherhells, which he'd use to frighten off anyone who stood in the way of his plans."

She turned and looked at the dragon. "Luckily, one of those creatures was Hubert."

"Alea! How could you? Betrayed!" The duke clutched at his heart. "My own daughter!"

"Come, Father. What you're doing is dangerous and wrong. Your greed will make a monster of you. I've been worrying what my future was with you and the castle. But now I know." She glanced happily back to the dragon. "Hubert and I have decided to go on the stage."

The duke was taken aback.

"What?"

"Yes, good sir," Hubert the dragon remarked. "I have some small experience in the field and on talking with your daughter, have found that she is just the partner I have been looking for."

"Yes, Father. A life on the stage. How much better than sitting around a tiny castle, waiting to be rescued by a clumsy young man."

Clumsy? My world reeled around me. Not wishing to be rescued was one thing, considering the situation. But to call me clumsy? I lowered my staff and walked toward the door.

"Wait!" my secret love cried. I turned quickly. Perhaps she had reconsidered her harsh words. Our long afternoons together still meant something!

"You haven't seen our act!" she exclaimed. "Hit it, dragon!"

She danced back and forth across the castle floor, the dragon beating time with its tail. They sang together:

> "Let's raise a flagon
> For damsel and dragon,
> The best song and dance team in the whole,
> wide world.
> Our audience is clapping,
> And their toes are tapping,
> For a handsome reptile and a pretty girl!"

The dragon blew smoke rings at the end of a line and breathed a bit of fire at the end of a verse. Six more verses followed, more or less the same. Then they stopped singing and began to shuffle back and forth.

They talked in rhythm.

"Hey, dragon. It's good to have an audience again."

"I'll say, damsel. I'm all fired up!"

They paused.

"How beautiful it is in Gurnish Keep! What more could you ask for, damsel, than this kind of sunny day?"

"I don't know, dragon. I *could* do with a shining knight!"

They paused again.

"Romance among reptiles can be a weighty problem!"

"Why's that, dragon?"

"When I see a pretty dragoness, it tips my scales!"

They launched into song immediately.

"*Let's raise a flagon*
For damsel and dragon—"

"I can't stand it anymore!" the Duke of Gurnish cried. "Slabyach! Grimace! Trolls, get them all!"

A trapdoor opened in the corner of the castle floor. The trolls popped out.

"Quick, Wunt!" Ebenezum cried. "Out of the way!" But before he could even begin to gesture, he was caught in a sneezing fit.

The trolls sauntered toward us. I bopped one on the head with my staff. The staff broke.

"Slobber!" exclaimed the troll.

"Roohhaarrr!" came from across the room. The dragon stood as well as it was able in the confines of the castle's great hall. It carefully directed a thin lance of flame toward each troll's posterior.

"No slobber! No slobber!" the trolls exclaimed, escaping back through the trapdoor.

"Thank you," Ebenezum said after blowing his nose. "That was quite nice of you."

"Think nothing of it," the dragon replied. "I never sacrifice an audience."

"I finally got our good Lord of Gurnish to listen to reason," my master said when we returned to our cottage. "When I mentioned how close to the palace I might be soon, and that I might find myself discussing the region, the duke saw his way to hire me as a consultant." Ebenezum pulled a jangling pouch from his belt. "The duke will now most likely receive clearance to build his tollbooths. Pity he no longer has the money for their construction."

"And what of his daughter and the dragon?" I asked.

"Hubert is flying the two of them to Vushta this very instant. I gave them a letter of introduction to certain acquaintances I have there, and they should find a ready audience."

"So you think they're that good?"

Ebenezum shook his head vigorously. "They're terrible. But the stage is a funny thing. I expect Vushta will love them."

"But enough of this." The wizard drew another, smaller pouch from his bag. "Hubert was kind enough to lend me some ground dragon's egg. Seems it's a folk remedy among his species; gives quick, temporary relief. I've never found this particular use for it in any of my tomes, but I've tried everything else. What do I have to lose?"

He ground the contents of the pouch into a powder and dropped it in a flagon of wine.

"This might even save us a trip to Vushta." He held his nose and lifted the concoction to his lips. My hopes sank as he drank it down. With Alea gone, a trip to Vushta was the only thing I had to look forward to.

The wizard opened a magical tome and breathed deeply. He smiled.

"It works! No more sneezing!"

His stomach growled.

"It couldn't be." A strange look stole over the wizard's face. He burped.

"It is! No wonder I couldn't find this in any of the tomes! I should have checked the *Netherhell Index*! It's fine for dragons, but for humans . . ." He paused to pull a book from the shelf and leaf rapidly through it. He burped again. His face looked very strained as he turned to me.

"Neebekenezer's Syndrome of Universal Flatulence!" he whispered. A high, whining sound emerged from his robes.

"Quick, Wunt!" he cried. "Remove yourself, if you value your sanity!"

I did as I was told. Even from my bed beneath the trees, I could hear the whistles, groans, and muffled explosions all night long.

THREE

"Every sorcerer should explore as much of the world as he can, for travel is enlightening. There are certain circumstances, such as a major spell gone awry, or an influential customer enraged at the size of your fee, where travel becomes more enlightening still."

—THE TEACHINGS OF EBENEZUM, Volume V

Thus we were forced, at last, to leave our cottage and seek outside assistance. My master realized he could not cure his own affliction—the first time, I think, that the wizard had to face up to such a circumstance. So we traveled to find another mage of sufficient skill and cunning, though we might have to travel to far Vushta, the city of a thousand forbidden delights, before we found another as great as Ebenezum.

The wizard walked before me along the closest thing to a path we could find in these overgrown woods. Every few paces he would pause, so that I, burdened with a pack stuffed with arcane and heavy paraphernalia, could catch up with his wizardly strides. He, of course, carried nothing.

Still, all was not right with my master. I saw it in his walk—the same long strides he always took, but something was missing: the calm placing of one foot in front of the other, knowing whatever lay in one's path, a wizard could handle it. He walked too swiftly now, anxious to be done with what I imagined he thought the most unsavory of tasks: asking another wizard for aid. It threatened to affect his whole bearing. For the first time in my apprenticeship, I worried for my master.

The wizard stopped midpath to gaze at the thick growth about us. "I will admit I'm worried, Wunt." He scratched at the thick white hair beneath his sorcerer's cap. "My maps and guidebooks indicated this was a lively area, with much commerce and no dearth of farms and friendly inns. That is the prime reason I took this route, for though we have cash from our recent exploits, a little more wouldn't hurt in the least."

The wizard stared out into the dark wood, his bushy eyebrows knitted in concern. "Frankly, I wonder now about the effectiveness of certain other preparations I made for our journey. You never know what you'll encounter when traveling."

There was a great crashing of underbrush to one side of the trail. Branches were rent asunder; leaves rustled and tore away; small forest creatures cried in fright.

"Doom!" cried someone from within the thicket. Something large fell between my master and myself. Ebenezum sneezed. There was sorcery in the air!

"Doom!" the voice cried again, and the dark

brown object that had fallen between us rose again. It was a tremendous club, I realized, for attached to the end nearest the thicket was a large hand, in turn attached to an arm that disappeared into the heavy greenery. Ebenezum fell back a few paces along the path and blew his nose on a wizardly sleeve, ready to conjure despite his affliction.

The club rose and fell repeatedly to crush the underbrush. A man appeared in the cleared space. He was enormous—well over six feet in height, with a great bronze helmet on his head, topped by ornamental wings that made him look even taller. And he was almost as wide as he was tall, his stomach covered by armor of the same dull bronze.

He stepped out to block our path. "Doom!" his deep voice intoned once more. Ebenezum sneezed.

There was no helping it. I dropped my pack and grabbed my stout oak staff in both hands. The armored man took a step toward the helplessly sneezing wizard.

"Back, villain!" I cried in a voice rather higher than I would have liked. Waving the staff above my head, I rushed the fiend.

"Doom!" the warrior intoned again. His barbed club met my staff in midair, shearing the sturdy oak in two.

"Doom!" The fiend swung once more. I ducked to avoid the blow and slipped on a pile of crushed leaves and vines littered beneath my feet. My left foot shot from under me, then my right. I fell into a bronze-plated belly.

"Doo—oof!" the warrior cried as he fell. His helmet struck the base of a tree, and he cried no more.

"Quick, Wunt!" Ebenezum gasped. "The club!"

He tossed a sack at my shoulder. I pushed myself

off the armored belly and managed to fit the cloth around the heavy weapon. The wizard let out a sigh and blew his nose.

"Enchanted."

So it was the club, and not the warrior, that had caused my master's sneezing attack. Ebenezum, once the greatest magician in all the forest country, now brought to this by his sorcerous affliction! The wizard leaned against a nearby tree, his breathing deep and ragged, as if his sneezes had robbed his lungs of air. I looked away until he might recover his breath, idly studying the pile of leaves into which I had fallen.

The warrior groaned where he lay.

"Quick, Wunt!" Ebenezum called. "Quit dawdling and tie the fellow up. I have a feeling we have much to learn from our rotund assailant."

The big man opened his eyes as I tightened the final knot on his wrists. "What? I'm still alive? Why haven't you killed and eaten me, the way demons usually do?"

"Indeed?" Ebenezum stared down at our captive, his eyes filled with wizardly rage. "And do we look like demons?"

The huge man paused. "Now that you mention it, not all that much. But you must be demons! It is my doom to always confront demons, my fate to fight them everywhere I turn, lest I be drawn into the Netherhells myself!" A strange light seemed to come into the large man's eyes, or perhaps it was only the quivering of his massive cheeks. "You could be demons in disguise! Perhaps you wish to torture me—slowly, exquisitely—with a cruelty known only to the Netherhells! Well, let's get it over with!"

Ebenezum stared at the quivering warrior for a

long moment, pushing his fingers through his great white beard. "I think the best torture would be to leave you talking to yourself. Wunt, if you'll shoulder your pack again?"

"Wait!" the stout man cried. "Perhaps I was hasty. You don't act like demons, either. And the way you felled me. A lucky blow to the stomach! You must be human! No demon could be that clumsy.

"Come, good fellows, I shall make amends!" He tugged at his hands, bound behind him. "But someone's tied me up!"

I assured him it was only a precaution. We thought he might be dangerous.

"Dangerous?" That look came into his eyes again, or perhaps it was the way his helmet fell to his eyebrows. "Of course I'm dangerous! I am the dread Hendrek of Melifox!"

He paused expectantly.

"You haven't heard of me?" he asked after neither one of us responded. "Hendrek, who wrested the enchanted warclub Headbasher from the demon Brax, with the promise it would be mine forever? The cursed Headbasher, which drinks the memories of men? It has given me such power, it has become a part of me! I need the club, despite its dread secret!"

His sunken eyes turned to the sack that held his weapon. "The demon did not inform me of the terms!" The warrior began to shake again. "No man can truly own Headbasher! They can only rent it! Twice a week, sometimes more, I am confronted by demons making demands. I must slay them, or do their fearsome bidding! For Brax did not tell me that when I won the club, I won it on the installment plan!" By now Hendrek shook uncontrollably, his armor clanking against his corpulent form.

"Installment plan?" mused Ebenezum, his interest suddenly aroused. "I had not thought the accountants of the Netherhells so clever."

"Aye, clever and more than that! Poor warrior that I am, I despaired of ever finding someone to save me from this curse, 'til I heard a song from a passing minstrel about the deeds of a great magician, Ebenezer!"

"Ebenezum," my master corrected.

"You've heard of him?" A cloud seemed to pass from before Hendrek's eyes. "Where can I find him? I am penniless, on the edge of madness! He's my last hope!"

I glanced at the wizard. Didn't the warrior realize?

"But he's—"

Ebenezum silenced me with a finger across his lips. "Penniless, did you say? You realize a wizard of his stature must charge dearly for his services. Of course, there is always barter—"

"But of course!" Hendrek cried. "You're a magician, too! Perhaps you can help me find him. I ask not only for myself, but for a noble cause—a curse that threatens the entire kingdom, emanating from the treasury of Melifox!"

"Treasury?" Ebenezum stood silent for a long moment, then smiled broadly for the first time since we began our journey. "Look no farther, good Hendrek. I am Ebenezum, the wizard of whom you speak. Come, we will free your treasury of whatever curse may have befallen it."

"And my doom?"

My master waved a hand of sorcerous dismissal. "Of course, of course. Wunt, untie the gentleman."

I did as I was told. Hendrek pushed himself erect and lumbered over to his club.

"Just leave that in the sack, would you?" Ebenezum called. "Just a sorcerous precaution."

Hendrek nodded and tied the sack to his belt.

I reshouldered my pack and walked over to my master. He seemed to have the situation well in hand. Perhaps my concern had been misplaced.

"What need have you to worry?" I asked in a low voice. "Minstrels still sing your praises."

"Aye," Ebenezum whispered back. "Minstrels will sing anyone's praises for the right fee."

The warrior Hendrek led us through the thick underbrush, which, if anything, became more impassable with every step. The late afternoon sun threw long shadows across our paths, making it difficult to see exactly where you placed your feet, which made the going slower still.

As we stumbled through the darkening wood, Hendrek related the story of the curse of Krenk, capital city of the kingdom of Melifox, and how demons roamed the city, making it unsafe for human habitation, and how all the land around the capital grew wild and frightening, like the woods we passed through now. How Krenk had two resident wizards, neither of whom had been able to lift the curse, so that, as a last resort, Hendrek had struck a bargain for an enchanted weapon but had failed to read the infernally small print. But then their ruler, the wise and kind King Urfoo the Brave, heard a song from a passing minstrel about a great wizard from the forest country. Hendrek had been sent to find that wizard, at any cost!

"Any cost?" Ebenezum echoed. His step had

regained the calm dignity I was more familiar with,
not even faltering in the bramble patch we were now
traversing.

"Well," Hendrek replied, "Urfoo has been known
to exaggerate slightly on occasion. I'm sure, though,
that as you're the last hope of the kingdom, he'll—"

Hendrek stopped talking and stared before him.
We had reached a solid wall of vegetation, stretching
as far as the eye could see and a dozen feet above our
heads.

"This wasn't here before," Hendrek muttered. He
reached out a hand to touch the dense, green wall. A
vine snaked out and encircled his wrist.

Ebenezum sneezed.

"Doom!" Hendrek screamed, and pulled his great
club Headbasher from the sack at his belt.

Ebenezum sneezed uncontrollably.

Hendrek's club slashed at the vine, but the greenery bent with the blow. The whole wall was alive
now, a dozen vines and creepers waving in the air.
They reached for Hendrek's massive form. His
swinging club pushed them back. Ebenezum hid his
head in his voluminous robes. Muffled sneezing
emerged from within the folds.

Something grabbed my ankle: a brown vine, even
thicker than those that threatened Hendrek, winding
up my leg toward my thigh. I panicked and tried to
leap away, but I only succeeded in losing my footing.
The vine dragged me toward the unnatural wall.

Hendrek was there before me, slashing in the midst
of the gathered green. His strokes were weaker than
before, and he no longer cried out. Vines encircled
his form, and it was only the matter of a moment
before he was lost to the leafage.

I yanked again at the creeper that held me captive.

It still held fast, but I caught a glimpse of my master behind me as I was dragged the last few feet to the wall.

The vines were all about the wizard, but only pushed at his sorcerous robes, as if the animate vegetation somehow sensed that Ebenezum was a greater threat than either Hendrek or myself. A gnarled tendril crept toward the wizard's sleeve, groping for his exposed hand.

Ebenezum flung the robes away from his face and made three complex passes in the air, uttering a dozen syllables before he sneezed again. The tendril at his sleeve grew brown and withered, dissolving into dust.

My leg was free! I kicked the dead vine away and stood. Ebenezum blew his nose heartily on his sleeve. Hendrek had collapsed in what had been the vegetable wall. Leaves crackled beneath him as he gasped for air.

"Doom!" Hendrek groaned as I helped him to his feet. "'Tis the work of demons, set on exacting vengeance upon me for nonpayment!"

Ebenezum shook his head. "Nonsense. 'Twas nothing more than sorcery. A simple vegetable aggression spell, emanating from Krenk, I imagine." He started down the newly cleared path. "Time to be off, lads. Someone, it appears, is expecting us."

I gathered up my gear as quickly as possible and trotted after Ebenezum. Hendrek took up the rear, muttering even more darkly than before. I saw what looked like a city before us on a distant hill, its high walls etched against the sunset sky.

We reached the walls sometime after nightfall. Hendrek pounded on the great oak gate. There was no response.

"They fear demons," Hendrek said in a low voice. Rather more loudly, he called: "Ho! Let us in! Visitors of importance to the township of Krenk!"

"Says who?" A head, clad in an ornate silver helmet, appeared at the top of the wall.

"Hendrek!" intoned the warrior.

"Who?" the head replied.

"The dread Hendrek, famed in song and story!"

"The dread who?"

The warrior's hand clutched convulsively at the sack that held the club. "Hendrek, famed in song and story, who wrested the doomed club Headbasher—"

"Oh, Hendrek!" the head exclaimed. "That large fellow that King Urfoo the Brave sent off on a mission the other day!"

"Aye! So open the gates! Don't you recognize me?"

"You do bear a passing resemblance. But one can't be too careful these days. You look like Hendrek, but you might be two or three demons, huddled close together."

"Doom!" Hendrek cried. "I must get through the gate, to bring the wizard Ebenezum and his assistant before the king!"

"Ebenedum?" The head's voice rose in excitement. "The one the minstrels sing about?"

"Ebenezum," my master corrected.

"Yes!" Hendrek roared back. "So let us in. There are demons about!"

"My problem exactly," the head replied. "The two others could be demons, too. With the three huddled together to masquerade as Hendrek, that would make five demons I'd be letting through the gate. One can't be too careful these days, you know."

Hendrek threw his great winged helmet to the ground. "Do you expect us to stand around here all night?"

"Not necessarily. You could come back first thing in the mornin—" The head's suggestion was cut short when it was swallowed whole by some large green thing that glowed in the darkness.

"Demons!" Hendrek cried. "Doom!" He pulled his warclub from the sack. Ebenezum sneezed violently. Meanwhile, up on the parapet, a second thing had joined the first. This one glowed bright pink.

What appeared to be an eye floating above the circular green glow turned to regard the pink thing, while the eye above the pink turned to look at the green. Something dropped from the middle of the green mass and writhed its way toward us down the wall. A similar tentacle came from the pink creature to grab the green appendage and pull it back up the wall. Both orbs grew brighter with a whistling sound that rose and rose, then both vanished with a flash and a sound like thunder.

The door to the city opened silently before us.

The wizard turned away from Hendrek and blew his nose.

"Interesting city you have here," Ebenezum said as he led the way.

There was something waiting for us inside. Something about four and a half feet high, its skin a sickly yellow. It wore a strange suit of alternate blue and green squares, as if someone had painted a chessboard across the material. A piece of red cloth was tied in a bow around its neck. There were horns on its head and a smile on its lips.

"Hendrek!" the thing cried. "Good to see you again!"

"Doom!" the warrior replied as he freed his club from his sack. Ebenezum stepped away and held his robes to his nose.

"Just checking on my investment, Henny. How do you like your new warclub?"

"Spawn of the Netherhells! Headbasher will never be yours again!"

"Who said we wanted it? Headbasher is yours—for a dozen easy payments! And nothing that costly. A few souls of second-rate princes, the downfall of a minor kingdom, a barely enchanted jewel or two. Then the wondrous weapon is truly yours!"

The creature deftly dodged the swinging warclub. Cobblestones flew where the club hit the street.

"And what a weapon it is!" the demon continued. "The finest warclub to ever grace our showroom! Did I say used? Let's call it previously owned. This creampuff of a weapon sat in the arsenal of an aged king, who only used it on Sunday to bash in the heads of convicted felons. Thus its colorful name, and its beautiful condition. Take it from me, Smilin' Brax" —the demon fell to the pavement as Headbasher whizzed overhead—"there isn't a finer used club on the market today. As I was saying just the other day to my lovely—urk—"

The demon stopped talking when I hit it on the head. I had managed to sneak up behind the creature as it babbled and knocked it with a rather large cobblestone. The creature's blue-and-green-checked knees buckled under the blow.

"Easy terms!" it gasped.

Hendrek quickly followed with a blow from Headbasher. The demon ducked, but it was still groggy from the first blow. The club caught its shoulder.

"Easy payments!" the thing groaned.

Hendrek's club came down squarely on the sickly yellow head. The demon's smile faltered. "This may be—the last time—we make this special offer!" The creature groaned again and vanished.

Hendrek wiped the yellow ichor off Headbasher with a shabby sleeve. "This is my doom," he whispered hoarsely, "to be forever pursued by Smilin' Brax, with his demands for Headbasher, which no man can own, but can only rent!" That strange light seemed to come into his eyes again, though perhaps it was only the reflection of the moon on the cobblestones.

Ebenezum stepped from the shadows. "It doesn't seem as bad as all that. . . . Uh, put that club back in the sack, would you? That's a good mercenary, mustn't take any chances." He blew his nose. "The two of you defeated the demon tidily."

My master pulled his beard reflectively. "As I see it, the effectiveness of any curse depends on how the cursed looks at it. Watching the proceedings very carefully, with a wizard's trained eye, mind you, I can state categorically that once we disenchant the treasury, you'll have nothing to worry about."

A weight seemed to lift from Hendrek's brow. "Really?"

"You may depend on it." Ebenezum brushed at his robes. "Incidentally, does good King Urfoo really consider us the last hope for rescuing his gold?"

Hendrek assured us once again of the importance of our quest, then proceeded to lead us through the winding streets of Krenk to Urfoo's castle. I'd grown up in the duchy of Gurnish, in and around Wizard's Woods, and Krenk was the largest town I had ever seen, with walls and a gate, as many as five hundred buildings, even paved streets! But I saw nothing else

as we walked. Where were the taverns, where we
could stop and exchange pleasantries with the
natives? Where were the town's attractive young
women? How could I be prepared when we finally arrived in Vushta, the city of a thousand forbidden
delights, if every town was as dead as this?

There was a scream in the distance. Hendrek froze,
but the scream was followed by a woman's laughter.
At least some were enjoying themselves, I supposed.
Was the whole town so afraid of demons?

We came to an open space, in the middle of which
was a building twice as grand and five times as large
as anything around it. There was a guard standing in
front of the palace's huge door, the first human we'd
seen since entering Krenk.

"Halt!" the guard cried as we walked into the
courtyard before him. "And be recognized!"

Hendrek kept on moving. "Important business
with King Urfoo!"

The guard unsheathed his sword. "Identify
yourself, under penalty of death!"

"Doom!" the immense warrior moaned. "Don't
you recognize Hendrek, back from an important mission for the king?"

The guard squinted in the darkness. "Don't I
recognize who? I didn't quite catch the name."

"The dread Hendrek, here with the wizard
Ebenezum!"

"Ebenezus? The one they all sing about?" The
guard bowed in my master's direction. "I'm honored, sir, to meet a wizard of your stature."

The guard turned back to Hendrek, who was quite
close to the door by now. "Now, what did you say
your name was again? I can't let just anybody

through this door. You can't be too careful these days, you know."

"Doom!" Hendrek cried, and with a speed amazing in one so large, he pulled his club from its restraining sack and bashed the guard atop the head.

"Urk," the guard replied. "Who are you? Who am I? Who cares?" The guard fell on his face.

"Headbasher, the club that drinks the memories of men. He will recover anon, but will remember none of this, or anything else, for that matter." Hendrek resheathed his club. "Come. We have business with Urfoo." He kicked the door aside and stormed into the castle.

I glanced at my master. He stroked his mustache for a moment, then nodded and said: "The treasury." We followed Hendrek inside.

We walked down a long hall. Sputtering torchlight made our shadows dance against huge tapestries that covered the walls. A breeze from somewhere blew against my coat to make me feel far colder than I had outside. This, I realized, was the castle with the curse.

Two guards waited before a door hung with curtains at the far end of the hall. Hendrek bashed them both before either could say a word.

Hendrek kicked this door open as well.

"Who?" a voice screamed from the shadow of a very large chair on a raised platform in the room's center.

"Hendrek," the warrior replied.

"Who's that?" A head sporting a crown peered over the arm of the great chair. "Oh, yes, that portly fellow we sent off last week. What news, what?"

"I've brought Ebenezum."

There was a great rustling as people rose from their hiding places around the room. "Nenebeezum?" someone said from behind a chair. "Ebenezix?" came a voice from behind a pillar.

"Ebenezum," replied my master.

"Ebenezum!" a chorus of voices responded as a good two dozen people stepped from behind marble columns, tapestries, and suits of armor to stare at my master.

"The Ebenezum? The one they sing about?" King Urfoo sat up straight in his throne and smiled. "Hendrek, you shall be justly rewarded!" The smile fell. "Once we take the curse off the treasury, of course."

"Doom," Hendrek replied.

King Urfoo directed us to sit on cushioned chairs before him, then paused to look cautiously at the room's shadow-hung corners. Nothing stirred. The ruler coughed and spoke. "Best get down to business, what? One can't be too careful these days."

"My thoughts exactly, good king." Ebenezum rose from his seat and approached the throne. "I understand there is a cursed treasury involved? There's no time to waste."

"Exactly!" Urfoo glanced nervously at the rafters overhead. "My money involved too. Lovely money. No time to waste, what? I'd best introduce you now to my two sorcerous advisers."

Ebenezum stopped his forward momentum. "Advisers?"

"Yes, yes, the two court wizards. They can fill you in on the details of the curse." Urfoo tugged a chord by his side.

"I generally work alone." My master pulled at his

beard. "But when there's a cursed treasury involved, I suppose one can adjust."

A door opened behind the king and two robed figures emerged, one male, one female. "No time to waste!" the king exclaimed. "May I introduce you to your colleagues, Granach and Vizolea?"

The newcomers stood on either side of Urfoo's throne, and for an instant, the three wizards regarded each other in silence. Then Vizolea smiled and bowed to my master. She was a tall, handsome woman of middle years, almost my height, red hair spiced with gray, strong green eyes, white teeth showing in an attractive smile.

Ebenezum returned the gesture with a flourish.

Granach, an older man dressed in gray, nodded to my master in turn, something on his face half smile, half grimace.

"The problem," King Urfoo said, "is demons, of course." He cringed on the word "demons," as if he expected one of them to strike him down for mentioning their existence. "We're beset with them. They're everywhere! But mostly"—he pointed a quivering hand toward the ceiling, "they're in the tower that holds the treasury!"

He lowered his hand and took a deep breath.

"Doom," Hendrek interjected.

"But perhaps," the king continued, "my court wizards can give you a better idea of the sorcerous fine points." He glanced quickly to either side.

"Certainly, my lord," Granach said quickly behind his half grimace. "Although none of this would have been necessary if we used the Spell of the Golden Star."

Urfoo sat bolt upright. "No! That spell would cost

me half my funds! There has to be a better way. Doesn't there?''

Ebenezum stroked his mustache. "Most assuredly. If the other wizards are willing to discuss the situation with me, I'm sure we can find some solution."

"Nothing's better than the Golden Star!" Granach snapped.

"Half my gold!" the king cried. He added in a whisper: "Perhaps you should all—uh . . . inspect the tower?"

Granach and Vizolea exchanged glances.

"Very good, my lord," Vizolea replied. "Do you wish to accompany us now?"

"Accompany you?" Urfoo's complexion grew paler still. "Is that completely necessary?"

Vizolea nodded, a sad smile on her face. "For the hundredth time, yes. It states directly in the sorcerer's charter that a member of the royal family must accompany all magicians on visits to the treasury."

"Signed right there," Granach added. "At the bottom of the page. In blood."

Urfoo pushed his crown back to mop his brow. "Oh, dear. How could that have happened?"

"If you'll excuse me for mentioning it, my lord," Vizolea said with downturned eyes, "'twas you who stipulated the terms of the pact."

The king swallowed. "There is no time to waste. I must accompany you?"

Granach and Vizolea nodded. "There's no helping it, without the Golden Star," Granach added.

"And so you shall!" My master's voice broke through the tension around the throne. "We shall inspect the treasury, first thing in the morning!"

Urfoo, who had been slowly sinking in his throne, sat up again and smiled. "Morning?"

Ebenezum nodded. "My 'prentice and I have just completed a long journey. How much better to confront a curse during the light of day with a clear head!"

"Morning!" Urfoo the Brave shouted. He smiled at the court-appointed wizards. "You are dismissed until breakfast, what? Ebenezum, I can tell you are a wizard of rare perception. I shall have my serving girls make your beds and bring you dinner. And in the morning, you will end the curse!"

I sat up straight myself. Serving girls? Perhaps there was something of interest in the township of Krenk after all.

"We must plan, Wunt," my master said when we were at last alone. "We only have 'til morning."

I turned from arranging the pile of cushions and skins that I was to sleep on. My master sat on a large bed they had provided him, head in hands, one on either side of his beard.

"I did not expect wizards." He threw his cap on the bed then and stood. "But the accomplished mage must be prepared for every eventuality. It is of utmost importance, especially concerning the size of our fee, that no one should learn of my unfortunate malady."

The sorcerer paced across the room. "I shall instruct you on certain items that have been stored in your pack. We must keep up appearances. And the business with that warrior's enchanted club has given me an idea. We'll best my affliction yet."

There was a knock on the door.

"I was expecting that," Ebenezum said. "See which one it is."

I opened the door to find Granach. He shuffled into the room, still wearing his grimace smile.

"Excuse me for interrupting at so late an hour," the gray-clad wizard began, "but I did not feel earlier that I had an opportunity to welcome you properly."

"Indeed," Ebenezum replied, raising one bushy eyebrow.

"And I thought there were certain things that you should be informed of. Before we actually visit the tower, that is."

"Indeed?" Both eyebrows rose this time.

"Yes. First, a quick word about our patron, King Urfoo the Brave. It is fortunate for him that the Krenkites prefer epithets added early during a ruler's reign, for since he gave up chasm-jumping at the age of sixteen, Urfoo has spent all his time in the treasury tower, counting his gold. Note that I didn't mention spending. Just counting. If you were anticipating a large return on your services, you might as well leave now. Our ruler should rather be called King Urfoo the Stingy. The payment won't be worth the risk!"

"Indeed." Ebenezum stroked his beard.

Granach coughed. "Now that you know, I expect you'll be on your way."

My master tugged the creases of his sleeves into place. "Indeed, no. A traveling magician, unfortunately, cannot pick and choose his clients in the same way a town mage might. He has to accept what tasks come his way, and hope that what small payment he might receive will be enough to take him farther on his journey."

The toothy grimace disappeared completely from

Granach's face. "You have been warned," he snarled from between tight lips. "The payment you will receive will in no way compensate for the danger you will face!"

Ebenezum smiled and walked to the door. "Indeed," he said as he opened it. "See you at breakfast?"

The other magician slithered out. Ebenezum closed the door behind him. "Now I'm sure there's money to be made here," he remarked. "But to business. I shall instruct you as to the proper volume and page number for three simple exorcism spells. I wonder, frankly, if we'll even need them."

He pulled one of the notebooks he was constantly writing in from his pocket and began to tear out pages. "In the meantime, I will begin to prepare my temporary remedy.

"The idea came from Hendrek's enchanted club." He tore the pages into strips. "When Hendrek's club is in the open air, I sneeze. However, when the club is in the sack, my nose is unaffected. It can no longer sense the club's sorcerous aroma. Therefore, if I stop my nasal sensitivity to things sorcerous, I should stop my sneezing!" He rolled the first of the strips into a tight cylinder. "But how to accomplish this, short of standing in the rain 'til I catch cold?"

He held the cylinder aloft so I could get a good look at it, then stuffed it up his nose.

There was another knock at the door.

"High time," Ebenezum said, pulling the cylinder back out. "See who it is this time, Wunt."

It was Vizolea. She had changed from her stiff wizard's robes into a flowing black gown with a low neckline. Her deep green eyes looked into mine, and she smiled.

"Wuntvor, isn't it?"

"Yes," I whispered.

"I would like to talk to your master, Ebenezum."

I stepped back to let her enter the room.

"I've always wanted to meet a wizard of your skill."

"Indeed?" my master replied.

She turned back to me, touched my shoulder with one long-fingered hand. "Wuntvor? Do you think you can leave your master and me alone for a while?"

I glanced at the mage. He nodded rapidly.

"Let me tell you about the Golden Star," Vizolea said as I closed the door behind me.

I stood in the hallway outside the room for a moment, stunned. I had a feeling from Vizolea's manner that she wanted to do more than talk. With my master? I had been known, in recent months, to keep company with a number of young ladies in my home district, but somehow Ebenezum had always seemed above that sort of thing.

But I was still only an apprentice, unaware of the nuances of a true sorcerer's life. I sat heavily, wondering how I could get to sleep on the hallway's cold stone floor, and wishing, for just a moment, that a serving maid of my very own might wander by and make my situation more comfortable.

She wanted to leave.

Wait! I cried. I'm a sorcerer's apprentice. When will you get another chance to dally with anyone half as interesting?

She wouldn't listen. She drifted farther and farther away. I ran after her, trying to shorten the distance.

It was no use. She was oblivious to me. I grabbed at her lowcut serving gown, pushed the tray from her hands, begged her to give me a single word.

"Doom," she said in far too low a voice.

I awoke to see Hendrek's face, lit by torchlight.

"Beware, Wuntvor! 'Tis not safe to sleep in these halls! Demons roam them in the wee hours!" He leaned close to me, his overstuffed cheeks aquiver, and whispered: "You moaned so in your sleep, at first I thought you were a demon, too!"

I saw then he held Headbasher in his free hand. "Some nights I cannot sleep, I fear the demons so. 'Tis strange, though. Tonight I've seen nary a one. Grab on to my club!" He helped me to my feet. "What brings you to moans in the hallway?"

I explained my dreams of serving maids.

"Aye!" Hendrek replied. "This place is full of haunted dreams. This cursed palace was built by Urfoo's doomed grandfather—some called him Vorterk the Cunning, others called him Mingo the Mad. Still others called him Eldrag the Offensive, not to mention those few who referred to him as Greeshbar the Dancer. But those are other stories. I speak now of the haunted corridors Vorterk built. Sound will sometimes carry along them for vast distances, seemingly from a direction opposite to where it actually originates. Hush, now!"

I didn't mention that it was he who did all the talking, for there was indeed a voice in the distance, screaming something over and over. I strained to hear.

It sounded like "Kill Ebenezum! Kill Ebenezum! Kill Ebenezum!"

"Doom!" Hendrek rumbled. I took a step in the direction of the screams. Hendrek grabbed my coat in his enormous fist and dragged me the other way through the maze of corridors. He paused at each intersection for a fraction of a moment, waiting for the screams to tell him which way to turn. Sometimes it seemed we turned toward the sounds, other times away. I became lost in no time at all.

But the voices were clearer now. There were two of them, and the one no longer shouted. Both were agitated, though.

"I don't think so."

"But we have to!"

"You want to move too fast!"

"You don't want to move at all! We'll have to wait for years before we get the treasury!"

"If I let you handle it, it will slip through our fingers! We should enlist Ebenezum!"

"No! How could we trust him? Ebenezum must die!"

"Perhaps I should join Ebenezum and do away with you!"

Hendrek stopped suddenly and I walked into him. His armor banged against my knee.

"There's someone out there!"

A door was flung open just before us. I froze, waiting for the owners of the voices to emerge.

Something else came out instead.

"Doom," Hendrek muttered when he saw it crawl our way. It looked like a spider, except that it was as large as me and had a dozen legs rather than eight. It was also bright red.

Hendrek swung the club above his head. Headbasher looked far smaller than it had before.

The creature hissed and jumped across the hall. Something else followed it out of the room. Large and green, the newcomer looked something like a huge, bloated toad with fangs. It jumped next to the spider-thing and growled in our direction.

"Doom, doom," Hendrek wheezed. I considered running, but Hendrek's bulk blocked my only escape route.

The bloated toad leapt in front of the almost spider. Its fangs seemed to smile. Then the red, many-legged thing scuttled over it in our direction. The toad growled and pushed past the dozen legs, but four legs wrapped around the toad and flipped it over. The almost spider moved in front.

Then the toad-thing jumped straight on top of the many-legged red thing. The almost spider hissed, the toad-thing growled. Legs interlocked, they rolled. Soon we could see nothing but flashing feet and dripping fangs.

Both disappeared in a cloud of brown, foul-smelling smoke.

"Doom," Hendrek muttered.

Another door opened behind us.

"Don't you think it was time you were in bed?"

It was Ebenezum.

I started to explain what had happened, but he motioned me to silence. "You need your sleep. We've a big day tomorrow." He nodded at Hendrek. "We'll see you in the morning."

The warrior looked once more at the spot where the creatures had disappeared. "Doom," he replied, and walked down the hall.

"Not if I can help it," Ebenezum said as he closed the door.

FOUR

" 'Never trust another sorcerer' is a saying un-
fortunately all too common among magical
practitioners. Actually, there are many instances
where one can easily trust a fellow magician,
such as cases where no money is involved, or
when the other mage is operating at such a
distance that his spells can't possibly affect
you."

—THE TEACHINGS OF EBENEZUM, Volume XIV

No one ate when we met for breakfast. I sat quietly,
running the three short spells I had memorized over
and over in my head. My master was quieter than
usual, too, being careful not to dislodge the thin rolls
of paper that packed his nose. Vizolea and Granach
glared at each other from opposite sides of the table,
while Hendrek muttered and the king quivered.

Ebenezum cleared his throat and spoke with the
lower half of his face. "We must inspect the tower."
His voice sounded strangely hollow.

"The tower?" Urfoo whispered. "Well, yes, there's no time to lose." He swallowed. "The tower."

Ebenezum stood. The rest followed. "Hendrek," my master instructed, "lead the way."

The mage strode over to the king. "As we go on our inspection, Your Majesty, I should like to discuss the matter of our fee."

"Fee?" Urfoo quivered. "But there's no time to lose! The treasury is cursed!"

Vizolea was by my master's side. "Are you sure you really wish to inspect the tower? There may be things there you do not want to see." Her hand brushed his shoulder. "You do remember our conversation last night?"

"Indeed." Ebenezum tugged his mustache meaningfully. "I have a feeling there are things about this treasury that will surprise us all."

"Doom!" came from the front of the line as the procession moved from the throne room.

"Do I really have to come along?" came from the end.

"The charter," Granach replied.

"Perhaps we *are* being a bit hasty, what?" The king wiped his brow with an ornate lace sleeve. "What say we postpone this, to better consider our options?"

"Postpone?" Granach and Vizolea looked at each other. "Well, if we must."

They turned and started back for the great hall.

"If you postpone this," Ebenezum said as he caught the eye of the king, "King Urfoo may never see his money again."

"Never?" The king positively shook. "Money?

Never? Money? Nevermoney?" He took a deep
breath. "No time to lose, what? To the tower!"

We climbed a narrow flight of stairs to a large
landing and another thick oak door.

"The treasury," Hendrek intoned.

"Your Majesty. The incantation, if you would,"
Granach remarked.

Urfoo huddled in the rear corner of the landing,
eyes shut tight, and screamed:

> "Give me an O! O!
>   Give me a P! P!
>   Give me an E! E!
>   Give me an N! N!
>   What's that spell?
>   Open! Open! Open!"

The door made a popping noise and did as it was
bidden. No sound came from within.

"Go ahead," Urfoo called. "I'll just wait out
here."

Ebenezum strode into the treasury.

The room was not large, but it was not particularly
small, either. And it was filled with ornate boxes and
stacks of gold, fantastic jewelry, and quite a few un-
marked sacks, piled waist high at least, shoulder
height near the walls.

We waded into the midst of it.

"Doom," Hendrek murmured. "So where are the
demons?"

An unearthly scream came from the landing.
Urfoo entered, pursued by the spider.

"The Spider of Spudora!" my master cried. He
held his nose.

"Granach!" Vizolea exclaimed. "We didn't talk about this!"

"Your Majesty!" Granach shouted. "There is only one hope! The Golden Star, performed by me!"

"No, you don't!" Vizolea recited a few quick words beneath her breath. "If anyone recites the Golden Star, it will be me!"

The toad-thing hopped into the room.

"The Toad of Togoth!" my master said.

"Quick, Urfoo!" cried Granach. "Give me leave to perform the spell before it's too late!"

A red claw snapped out of a pile of jewels.

"The Crab of Crunz!" my master informed me.

"Not the crab!" Vizolea shrieked. "This time, Granach, you've gone too far! Bring on the Lice of Liftiana!"

Granach stepped aside to avoid the panting Urfoo, now pursued by the almost spider, the bloated toad, and a grinning crustacean.

"Oh, no, you don't!" the dour wizard cried. "Bring forth the dread Cows of Cuddotha!"

My master flung his hands in the air. "Stop this now! You'll cause a sorcerous overload!"

The air shimmered as the room was filled with a chorus of spectral moos. A sickly yellow form solidified before us.

"Ah, good Hendrek!" Smilin' Brax exclaimed. "How good to see you again. We of the demon persuasion like to check out areas of extreme sorcerous activity; see if we can do a little business, as it were. And boy, is there business here! Perhaps some of you folks would like to purchase an enchanted blade or two, before some of my folks arrive?"

"Doom," Hendrek muttered.

Urfoo ran past. "All right! All right! I'll think about the Golden Star!" A blue cow with bloodshot eyes galloped after him.

"The Lion of Lygthorpedia!"

"The Grouse of Grimola!"

"Stop it! Stop it! It's too much!" Ebenezum pulled back his sleeves, ready to conjure.

"How about you, lad?" Brax said to me. "I've got this nifty enchanted dagger, always goes straight for the heart. Makes a dandy letter opener, too. I'm practically giving it away. Just sign on this line down here."

"The Tiger of Tabatta!"

"The Trout of Tamboul!"

"Too much!" Ebenezum shouted, and sneezed the most profound sneeze I have ever seen. Paper showered over the newly materialized devil trout, while the force of the blow knocked Ebenezum back against a pile of jewels.

He didn't move. He had been knocked unconscious.

"Doom," Hendrek intoned.

"Then again," Brax said, looking around the room, "maybe I'd better sell you an axe."

"The Antelope of Arasaporta!"

Someone had to stop this! It was up to me. I had to use the exorcism spells!

"Sneebly Gravich Etoa Shrudu—" I began.

"The Elephant of Erasia!"

Wait a second. Was it "Sneebly Gravich Etoa" or "Etoa Gravich Sneebly"? I decided to try it the other way, too.

"All right! You force my hand! The Whale of Wakkanor!"

There was an explosion in the center of the room. Instead of a materialized whale, there was a lightless hole.

Ebenezum stirred on his bed of jewels.

Brax looked over his shoulder as the black void grew. "Drat. This would have to happen now, right on the edge of a sale. Oh, well, see you in the Netherhells!" The demon disappeared.

It was suddenly quiet in the room. The two other magicians had stopped conjuring, and all the demon creatures, crabs and cows, tigers and trout, had turned to watch the expanding hole.

Ebenezum opened his eyes. "A vortex!" he cried. "Quick! We can still close it if we work together!"

A wind rose, sucked into the hole. The creatures of the Netherhells, bats and rats, mice and lice, were drawn into the dark.

Granach and Vizolea both gestured wildly into the void.

"Together!" Ebenezum cried. "We must work together!" Then he began to sneeze. He pulled his robes to his nose, stepped back from the vortex. It was no use. He doubled over, lost to his malady.

The darkness was taking the jewels now, and the sacks of gold. And I could feel the wind pulling me. Granach screamed at it, and he was drawn in. Vizolea cried against it, then she was gone. The blackness reached out for Hendrek and the king, my master and me.

Ebenezum flung his robes away to shout a few words into the increasing gale. A bar of gold skidded by me and was swallowed. Ebenezum made a pass, and the vortex shrank. He gestured again, and the vortex grew smaller still, about the size of a man.

Then Ebenezum sneezed again.

"Doom!" Hendrek cried. King Urfoo, wide-eyed, was skidding across the floor to the void.

The warrior and I pushed against the wind to his aid. Jewels scattered beneath our feet and were lost. I shoved a chest toward the gaping maw, hoping to cover a part of it, but it was sucked straight through.

"My gold!" Urfoo cried as he rolled for the hole. I snagged a foot, Hendrek grasped the other. I struggled for footing on the loose jewels that rolled across the floor to the void. I slipped and fell into the warrior.

"Doo—oof!" he cried as he lost his balance. He fell back into the hole.

The wind stopped. Hendrek stood, half here and half somewhere else. His girth had plugged the vortex.

Ebenezum blew his nose. "That's better." He recited a few incantations, sneezed once more, and the hole sealed up as we pulled Hendrek free.

My master then gave a brief explanation to the king, who sat glassy-eyed on the now bare floor of the treasury. How his wizards had tried to cheat him of half the treasury by inventing a curse when they couldn't get the money any other way, thanks to the sorcerous charter that called for a member of the royal family to open the door. How Ebenezum had discovered this plot, and how he should be amply rewarded for saving the king's money.

"Money?" King Urfoo the Brave whispered as he looked around. Perhaps a dozen jewels and gold pieces were left where once there had been a room of plenty. "Money! You've taken my money! Guards! Kill them! They've taken my money! Urk!"

Hendrek hit him on top of the head.

"They've—what? Where am I? Oh, hello." The king lost consciousness.

"Doom," Hendrek murmured. "Headbasher does its hellish job again."

My master suggested it might be a good time to travel.

We had to wait some hours in the pouring rain before we could get a ride away from Krenk. Ebenezum had thought it best, in case of pursuit, to cover his wizardly robes with a more neutral cloth of brown, and passing wagons were reticent to pick up characters as motley-looking as the three of us, especially with one the size of Hendrek.

"Perhaps," Ebenezum suggested with a pull on his beard, "we would have better luck if we separated."

"Doom!" Hendrek shivered and clutched at the bag that held Headbasher. "But what of my curse?"

"Hendrek." The wizard put a comradely hand on the large warrior's shoulder. "I can guarantee you'll see nothing of Brax for quite some time. The severity of that vortex was such that it shook through at least three levels of the Netherhells. Take it from an expert; their transportation lines won't be cleared for months!"

"Then," rumbled Hendrek, "I'm freed of Brax and his kind?"

"For the time being. Only a temporary remedy, I'm afraid. I have a certain affliction . . ." He paused, looking Hendrek straight in the eye. "Also temporary, I assure you, that keeps me from affecting a more permanent cure. However, I shall give you the names of certain sorcerous specialists in Vushta, who should be able to help you immediately." My master wrote three names on a page of his notebook and gave them to the warrior.

Hendrek thrust the piece of parchment in Head-basher's bag, then bowed low to my master. "Thank you, great wizard. To Vushta, then." His head seemed to quake with emotion, but perhaps it was only the rain pouring on his helmet.

"We're bound for Vushta ourselves, eventually," I added. "Perhaps we'll meet again."

"Who knows what the fates will?" said Hendrek as he turned away. "Doom."

He was soon lost in the heavy downpour.

Once the warrior was gone, I looked again to my master. He stood tall in the soaking rain, every inch a wizard despite his disguise. If any doubts had assailed Ebenezum on our arrival in Krenk, his actions in the subsequent events seemed to have erased them from his mind. He was Ebenezum, the finest wizard in all the forest country. And in Krenk as well!

Finally, I could bear it no longer. I asked my master what he knew about the plot against King Urfoo.

" 'Tis simple enough," Ebenezum replied. "Urfoo had the wealth that the wizards wanted, but couldn't get to, because of the charm on the door. So they devised the Spell of the Golden Star, through which, by their definition, Urfoo would have to release half the gold from the charmed tower in order for the spell to work. I don't blame them, in a way. According to Vizolea, the king hadn't gotten around to paying them in all the years they were in his service. Unfortunately, they got greedy, and didn't work in unison, and you saw what happened. They even considered working the Golden Star spell three ways; at

least Vizolea suggested as much, although"—my
master coughed—"I usually don't engage in such ac-
tivities."

He looked up and down the deserted road, then
reached in his damp coat to pull out a bar of gold.
"Good. I was afraid I'd lost it in our flight. I have so
many layers of clothing on, I could no longer feel it."

I gaped as he hid the gold again. "How did you get
that? The floor of the treasury was stripped."

"The floor was." The wizard nodded. "The in-
sides of my robes were not. A wizard has to plan
ahead, Wunt. Sorcerers are expected to maintain a
certain standard of living."

I shook my head. I should never have doubted my
master for a moment.

Ebenezum gazed off into the never-ending rain.
"Things are afoot, Wuntvor," he said after a moment's pause. "I had not thought we would find this
much sorcerous activity this soon."

"We've been lucky, then?" I asked.

"Perhaps. We were lucky, too, in the last few
months at our cottage. A half dozen high-paying
commissions, all somehow the result of the Netherhells. It has sent us on the road to Vushta far sooner
than I had imagined."

The wizard glared up at the sky. The water
splashed from his cheekbones and ran in rivulets
through his beard. "Oh, if I could risk a weather
spell! But I have sneezed far too much today. One
more sniff of magic tonight, and I fear my nose
would jump from my face."

My master made light of his malady, but still I
could tell it troubled him. I did my best to change the
subject.

"Tell me about Vushta," I said.

"Ah, Vushta, city of a thousand forbidden delights!" The wizard's mood seemed to lighten with every word. "If a man is not careful, the city might change him completely in the blink of an eye."

It was all I had been hoping for. I begged my master to go on.

"Let's hear no more of magic or fabled cities tonight," was all he would say. "Our luck holds with us. Methinks some sturdy tradesman has come to our rescue."

Indeed, a covered cart had pulled to the side of the road. Perhaps we would spend a dry and quiet night after all.

"Need a ride?" the driver called. We clambered in the back.

"'Tis a dismal night," the driver continued. "I'll sing you a song to lift your spirits. That's what I am—a traveling minstrel!"

Ebenezum looked out from his hood in alarm, then averted his face so that it was lost in shadow.

"Let's see what would be appropriate?" The minstrel tugged the reins of his mule. "Ah! Just the thing for a night straight from the Netherhells. I'll sing you a song about the bravest wizard around; fellow from the forest country up Gurnish way. Um . . . Neebednuzum, I think he's called. Now, this ditty's a little long, but I think you'll be struck by the fellow's bravery."

Ebenezum had fallen asleep by the third verse.

FIVE

"Your average ghost is a much more complex and interesting individual than is generally imagined. Just because someone is dragging chains or has one's head perpetually in flames does not necessarily make them of a lesser class. Some ghosts, especially those with heads attached and mouths to speak through, are actually quite good conversationalists, with other-worldly stories by the score. In addition, ghosts generally subscribe to the happy custom of disappearing completely at dawn, a habit many living associates and relatives might do well to cultivate."

—THE TEACHINGS OF EBENEZUM, Volume VI
(Appendix B)

After our harrowing experience with King Urfoo in Krenk, I think both Ebenezum and myself expected our luck to change. Perhaps we would at last find a wizard great enough to cure my master without having to travel to far Vushta.

But the city of a thousand forbidden delights began to seem more of a possibility with every passing day. What with being chased out of one kingdom and not being particularly welcome in the next two, we hadn't a chance to meet any wizards at all. Then there'd been the mercenaries Urfoo had sent to kill us, and the seven straight days of rain, and the incident with the giant swamp rats. I didn't even want to think of those.

But still my master walked on, proud and tall, toward far, forbidden Vushta. And I would follow him there, and anywhere. Even with his affliction, Ebenezum was the greatest wizard I had ever seen!

I touched my walking stick to my forehead in a silent salute to the man before me. Our luck was bound to change!

It was then that I lost my footing and slid down the hill, colliding with my master.

Our fall ended in a cluster of bushes at the valley bottom. Not looking at me, the wizard stood with a groan that was like the rumble of an approaching storm. He turned much too slowly to face me. I watched the eyes beneath bushy brows and waited for the inevitable.

"Wuntvor," the mage said, his voice like an earthquake splitting a mountainside. "If you can't watch where you put your—"

My master stopped midsentence and stared over my head. I began to stammer an apology, but the wizard waved me to silence.

"What do you hear, 'prentice?" he asked.

I listened but heard nothing. I told him so.

"Exactly," he replied. "Nothing at all. 'Tis the end of summer, deep in the wood, yet I do not see a single bird nor hear an insect. Though I must admit, the absence of the latter does not upset me over-much." The mage scratched at a pink welt beneath his long white beard. We had had a great deal of experience, ever since the seven days of rain, with clouds of mosquitoes and biting gnats.

"Methinks, Wunt, something is amiss."

I listened for a moment more. My master was right. The forest was silent, the only sounds the breathing of the wizard and myself. I had never heard quiet like this, except perhaps on the coldest days of winter. A chill went up my back, surprising in the late summer's heat.

My master dusted off his robes. "We seem to have landed near a clearing." He nodded down what remained of the hill. "Perhaps we shall find some habitation, even someone who can explain the nature of this place. Until then, we will bask in the absence of mosquitoes." He scratched his neck absently as he started down the hill. "Always look on the bright side, Wunt."

I hurriedly gathered up the foodstuffs, books, and magical paraphernalia that had fallen from my pack and followed my master's wizardly strides. I scrambled after him over the uneven ground, avoiding what underbrush there was. But the brush thinned rapidly as we walked, and we found ourselves facing a large clearing of bare earth, broken only by a ring of seven large boulders in its center.

"Now we've even lost the grasses," Ebenezum rumbled. "Come, Wunt, we'll find the cause of this." He took great strides across the bare ground, clouds of dust rising with every step. I followed close behind, doing my best not to cough.

When we reached the first boulder, something jumped.

"Boo!" the something said. I dropped my pack, but Ebenezum simply stood there and watched the apparition.

"Indeed," he said after a moment.

"Boo! Boo! Boo! Boo!" the creature confronting us shrieked. On closer inspection, I could see that it was definitely human, with long gray hair covering the face and brown rags concealing the body. The person raised frail hands and rushed us on unsteady legs.

Neither of us moved. Our attacker stopped, out of breath. "Not going to work, is it?" she wheezed at last. It was an old woman; her speaking voice was cracked and high.

Ebenezum stroked his mustache. "Is what not going to work?"

"Can't scare you away, huh?" She parted the long hair that covered her face and peered at the sky. "Probably too late for you to get away, anyhow. Might as well sit down and wait." She looked around for a likely rock and sat.

"Indeed," Ebenezum repeated. "Wait for what?"

"You don't know?" The woman's eyes widened in wonder. "Sir, you are in the dreaded Valley of Vrunge!"

"Indeed," Ebenezum said when it became apparent the woman planned to say no more.

"Now don't tell me you've never heard of it. What, do you come from the ignorant Western Kingdoms?" The woman laughed derisively. "Everyone knows of the Valley of Vrunge, and the dread curse that falls upon it once every one hundred and thirty-seven years. Not that this place is all that friendly at any time"—she spat on the parched earth—"but there is one night, every one hundred thirty-seven years, when all hell breaks loose. One night when no one then in the valley will get out alive!"

I didn't like the direction the woman's speech was taking. I swallowed hard and cleared my throat. "Ma'am, would you mind telling us just when that night is?"

"Haven't I made it clear?" The crone laughed again. "This is the cursed night of the Valley of Vrunge. It begins when the sun passes yonder hills." She pointed behind me.

I followed her arm and looked to the sun, already touching the top of the western hills, then turned to Ebenezum. He stared above me, lost in thought. It appeared our luck was running true to course.

"If we are all due to die," Ebenezum said at last, "what are you doing here?"

The old woman looked away from us. "I have my reasons, which I'm sure would be of little interest to anyone but me. Let us just say that once this land was green and fair, and it was ruled over by a princess as lovely as the land itself. But a dark time came upon the earth, and the sky rained toads, and the princess became afraid. But her suitor, the handsome—"

"You are quite right," Ebenezum interrupted. "No one would be interested in that at all. You've decided to die because the sky rained toads?"

The woman sighed and watched the sun disappear behind the hilltop. "Not exactly. I've worn this body out. I'm due to die. I just thought I'd see old Maggie out in style."

"Maggie?" Ebenezum scratched his insect bite thoughtfully. "That would be short for Magredel?" He peered into her ancient face.

"Oh, I haven't used that name in years. Not since I got away from those dull Western Kingdoms. Used to practice witchery thereabouts for a time, that's probably where you heard of me. Didn't specialize much, though. More of a general practitioner.''

"Maggie?" Ebenezum repeated. "As in old Aunt Maggie?"

Maggie squinted her eyes in turn. "Say, do I know you from someplace?"

There was an explosion directly behind me. All three of us spun to see a tall, pale apparition atop the tallest of the seven stones.

"Greetings, ladies and gentlemen!" the apparition cried with a swirl of its robe. "And welcome to curse night!"

"Greetings to you, too, Death," Maggie replied. "I hope tonight will be up to your usual standards?"

Death laughed, a high, echoey sound that came near to scaring the life out of me. When I mentioned it later to Ebenezum, he said that was no doubt the desired reaction.

The apparition atop the stone disappeared.

"That was our introduction," Maggie remarked. "Soon the fun begins."

I was appalled. "F-fun?" I stammered. "How do you know what happens next?"

"Simple." The crone flashed a toothless smile. "I've been through this night once before."

Now that Death had vanished, the silence was again complete. My master cleared his throat.

"Ebenezum!" the old woman cried. "Of course! I'd recognize that nervous cough anywhere. Poor little Ebby, always coughing or scratching or tugging or doing something. He never could sit still." She winked in my direction. "You know, in the whole first year he studied under me, he didn't get one spell straight? You should have seen the things that showed up in our kitchen!'' She laughed.

My master cast a worried glance at the rock where Death had stood. "Please, Aunt Maggie. I don't think this is the proper time to discuss—"

"Oh, keep your cap on!" The woman clapped Ebenezum on the shoulder. "We have a little time. It always takes them a while to get organized. When you only have one performance every one hundred thirty-seven years, you tend to get a bit rusty."

"But what's going to happen?" I asked. I noticed my hand hurt from my tight grip on my walking stick.

"Ghosts, ghosts, and more ghosts." The old woman spat on the ground. "Death is fond of games. He plays a game with every living thing, one in which he's always the victor. Some games he likes more than others, and those great conflicts he brings here, to play over and over again in the Valley of Vrunge!"

"The spirits just play games?" I asked. That didn't sound so bad.

"All of life is a game, remember. Death brings along the best of all his games, ranging from a nation at war to two people in love."

She jumped and screamed.

"Tickle, tickle, tickle," said a high voice from nowhere.

"Poltergeists! Boo! Boo! Boo! Away from here!" Maggie waved her hands about wildly. "More and more ghosts will appear throughout the night. And Death will try to snare you in his games. Beware, he always wins!" She screamed and jumped again.

"Boo, boo, boo?" the voice from nowhere asked. "That's passé, lady. These days, long, sensitive moans are much more the thing in ghostly circles."

"So it begins. I'm sorry, Ebby, you had to stumble

into this!'' She ran and screamed as "tickle, tickle tickle!" chased her around the circle of boulders.

Ebenezum sneezed once and blew his nose on a silver-inlaid sleeve. "Just a minor spirit. Hardly bothers me at all."

I realized then that this was the first time Ebenezum's malady had affected him since we entered the cursed valley. Perhaps the severity of our situation was effecting a cure. Ebenezum had not sneezed once in the presence of Death!

My master shook his head when I explained my theory. "Why should I sneeze? Death is the most natural thing in the world." He pulled at his beard. "And I fear that, should we fail to devise a plan of action, Death will become all too familiar to both of us."

A great wind sprang up. My master had to shout to be heard. "Stay close! If we're separated—"

The wizard sneezed as three ghosts on a sled grabbed him and whisked him high in the air. Ghosts, sled, and sneezing Ebenezum disappeared around the stones.

Night had fallen completely, and I was alone.

But then there was a crowd around me, sitting on long rows of seats, one atop another, as if they were built on a hillside. The crowd roared, and I saw they were watching a group of uniformed men on a green lawn, a few of whom were running, but most of whom were standing still.

A man carrying a big silver box walked up the steps toward me. "Hot dogs!" he cried. "Hot dogs!"

He wasn't real, I told myself. This whole place was beyond my understanding. I stepped aside to let him pass. He stopped next to me anyway.

"Hot dog, mister?"

It was only with a mental effort that I kept from shivering. I looked down at my stout oak staff. My grip was firm. If the apparition tried anything, I'd swing at him. And then again, from what I'd heard of ghosts, I might swing through him as well.

With some trepidation, I asked: "What's a hot dog?"

"Like I thought"—the spirit nodded sagely—"you're an outsider. So this is your first ball game? Well, you picked a good one, buddy."

I looked out over the field below us. "Ball game," I repeated, struggling to comprehend.

"Yeah," the apparition replied. "*The* ball game. People had counted the Red Sox out, but they came around. Now Torrez will blow the Yankees away! Seventy-eight is going to be our year. It *has* to be."

I looked closely at the spirit, hoping that some gesture or facial mannerism would help me to understand his ravings. All I saw was the haunted look, deep in his eyes.

"Has to be?" I asked.

"Well, yeah." The ghost paused. "I mean, the Sox have to win. Otherwise . . ." He shuddered. "Do you have any idea what it would be like to have to sell hot dogs throughout eternity?"

He didn't wait for an answer but walked up the stairs beyond me. I turned to the "ball game" on the field below. I felt a sudden, near overwhelming urge to be drawn into that game and find out just what could move the hot dog spirit to such a frenzy. I'd watch the shifting patterns of men on the bright green lawn, and sooner or later some great secret would be revealed, a joyous revelation that would make my whole existence take on new meaning!

Something in the back of my head told me to turn

away. I remembered Aunt Maggie's warning about Death and games.

The ball game disappeared. In its place stood Death.

"There you are," the creature said in his sonorous voice. "I've been looking all over for you. These curse evenings can be so long and boring, sometimes I like to indulge in games to help pass the time. Tell me, do you know how to play Red Light, Green Light?"

Death stood much closer than he had before. I stared at the thin layer of pale skin pulled tight over his skull, and at the shadows where there should have been eyes. Yet his smile was ingratiating. You wanted to believe in what he told you, rather like a good seller of used pack animals on market day.

"Well?" Death prompted.

"N-no!" I stammered. "I-I don't know the rules!"

"Oh, is that all." Death reached out to touch my arm. "I'll explain everything. I'm very good with rules."

"No! I have to find my master!" I pulled away from the creature's hand and ran blindly.

Suddenly a pit yawned before me. A pit filled with sharpened spikes and a great, roaring monster, all mouth and teeth and claws. I tried to stop, to step backward, but I was over the edge, falling, falling.

Someone barked a command behind me; my master's voice. I found myself on solid ground, standing by Ebenezum. All the ghosts were gone.

Ebenezum sneezed repeatedly, rocking with the force emitted by his nose.

"Temporary exorcism spell," he gasped at last. "Best I can manage."

I did a short jig on the parched earth while my master caught his breath. Ebenezum had freed himself from the sledding spirits! Hope once again rose within my breast.

I asked him how he'd accomplished his escape.

The wizard shrugged. "I sneezed my way free. The ghosts were ready for sorcery, a battle of wits, anything but extreme nasal activity. They simply evaporated before the onslaught of my nose."

"That's wonderful!" I cried. "We'll be free of this cursed valley in no time!"

Ebenezum shook his head. "Death does not make the same mistake twice. The next set of apparitions will be ready for my malady."

Aunt Maggie appeared around one of the seven great boulders. She staggered over to Ebenezum's feet and collapsed.

She groaned, then turned to look at my master. "It's gone! The poltergeist is gone!"

The wizard nodded solemnly. "Exorcism spell."

Maggie sighed in relief. "It kept taunting me, begging me to tickle it back. You can't give in to those things. It would have been all over." She looked at Ebenezum. "Exorcism? That means you followed your calling and graduated into wizardry! I did hesitate to ask you. In the early days, you were very determined, but your aptitude was sometimes less than—"

Ebenezum cleared his throat. "'Tis only a temporary spell. Death's power is greater than common magic, and the ghosts will push through presently. We must come up with a more permanent solution."

Maggie laughed. "I pulled through this cursed night once, with the aid of magic. Maybe we can do so again. And gain my kingdom back in the bargain!" She slapped my master's shoulder. "So one of my students made good? Let's see you do your stuff. Nothing fancy; a bird out of thin air, water into wine, something to catch an old woman's fancy."

Ebenezum fixed her with a wizardly stare. "We are in peril for our lives. I need to concentrate." He stalked off and disappeared into the circle of stone.

Maggie shook her head and smiled. "A great wizardly manner. He must be raking in the business." She sighed. "Wish I could work magic the way I used to. After a while, the body gives out. Can toss off a spell now and again, when I'm feeling spry. But the big ones are beyond my reach."

I hesitated to tell her that due to my master's affliction, just about all the spells that could save us from our present predicament were beyond his reach as well. Best not to upset her. I was upset enough for both of us.

"But let me tell you my story, and you'll understand why I'm here," she began. "You've already learned of the fair kingdom, and the beautiful princess. And then, of course, there were the raining toads. And did I tell you about the princess's handsome suitor, Unwin, killed on their wedding day? No? Well, that's a good place to—"

"Tickle, tickle, tickle," the disembodied voice chortled. The exorcism spell was over.

A cool breeze blew in my ear. "Hey, big boy," a woman whispered. "What's a fellow like you doing without a date on a night like this?"

I turned to gaze on the most beautiful apparition I had ever seen. I was speechless. She was slender and pale, with long silver hair. And she wore no clothing at all, ghostly or otherwise. At certain angles, you could see right through her, but at other angles she was more than my eyes could bear.

"Oh, the silent type," she said, and took my hand, her fingers intertwining with mine. Her touch was ice. It sent thrills up my arm and across my shoulders. She leaned close, and her breath was the breeze of autumn. Her lips parted, close to mine. I wanted to kiss those lips more than I wanted life itself.

"I know a little game we can play," the full, cool lips said. "It's called Spin the Bottle."

Yes, yes, whatever it was, yes! All those girls I'd known in the Western Kingdoms, even Alea, my afternoon beauty, they were nothing to me now.

But my beloved was pulled away from me and sent spinning through the air, her ectoplasm flying in every direction.

"I can still toss off a spell or two." Maggie smiled. "Got to watch out for succubi. Not good for your health."

"Crone!" Death was before us. "What would you know of love? Your body has been old and withered for a hundred years. An empty shell which can no longer be filled. Or can it?"

Death waved his hand and a young man materialized at his side.

"Unwin?" The old woman's voice was little more than a whisper. "Is that you, Unwin?"

"Magredel!" the young man cried. "What's happened to you?"

"It's not me, Unwin. It's you. You've been away. I haven't seen you in so long!"

The old woman was crying.

"Consider, woman," Death said. "Come with me

and you will be together always."

But Maggie turned on him, anger replacing sorrow. "No! You've stolen my kingdom for centuries! I'll be with Unwin soon enough! I must free what was tricked from me!"

"Such harsh words." Death examined his skeletal hand. "I have need of this place. My ghosts must have their exercise." He looked at me, and I shivered where I stood. "Come, Wuntvor. Let's leave these lovers alone while they talk things over. I'll give you the guided tour."

Without thinking, I found myself following him. Death smiled. "Simon says put your hands in the air."

It took all my willpower to keep my hands at my sides.

"We'll find one yet." Death's hands were full of small rectangles, which he fanned out before him. "How about a little Go Fish?"

I found myself staring at the rectangles. I looked the other way.

"My kingdom," Death said.

There were apparitions everywhere. Armies fighting, women laughing, people in costumes familiar and unfamiliar, crawling across the ground, climbing the trees, flying through the air in strange machines.

"Amazing," I said despite myself.

Death nodded. "The paperwork alone is staggering. Yet we pull it off, every one hundred thirty-seven years. It's a shame our audience has to be so small. The Vrunge Curse is my masterpiece. Here are all the greatest moments of humanity, past, present, future, played out over and over again, from men at war to men at play, games of chance to games of love. A pity. Perhaps I should advertise."

Death coughed gently. "Tell me, Wuntvor. Who is the greatest magician in all the Western Kingdom?"

Was he trying to trick me? I'd stay firm to my beliefs. "Why, Ebenezum, of course."

"Right!" Death cried as a gong sounded somewhere nearby. "Wuntvor, you've just won an additional five years on your life!"

We were surrounded by bright light. The ghosts all sat in a large amphitheater now, whistling and cheering. The succubus I had almost kissed stood a little bit to one side, next to a large board that read "5." She was wearing some sort of spangled costume that managed to look more revealing than her nudity had before.

"Okay!" Death smiled broadly. "Now, Wunt, for ten additional years! Tell us, who is the ruler of Melifox?"

The crowd whistled and stamped their feet. Urgent music came from somewhere. The succubus smiled her magnificent smile.

"Uh—King Urfoo the Brave!" I blurted.

"Right, for ten more years!"

The crowd went wild. The spangled beauty flipped a couple of cards over the board to one that read "15."

"All right! All right!" Death raised his hands for silence. "Now it's time for the question we've all been waiting for. Double or nothing!"

The crowd cheered.

"Now, Wuntvor, are you ready to double your life span?"

"Yes! Yes!" The crowd chanted. I nodded my head. Why not? This was easy.

"All right! The big question, Wuntvor, to double

your life span or erase it altogether! Who was the famous chamberlain of the Eastern Kingdoms, three centuries ago, who used to mutter to himself, " 'One of these days, one of these days'?"

"What?" I asked. How could I know something like that?

"Quick, Wuntvor! The Quiz Lady has set the clock. You have fifteen seconds to answer, or pay the penalty, on Forfeit Your Life!"

What? What could I do? I didn't know anything about the Eastern Kingdoms. The dramatic music was back, louder than ever. The crowd was roaring. I couldn't think. Why hadn't I listened to Maggie and kept away from these games?

"Ten!" the crowd chanted. "Nine! Eight! Seven! Six! Five!"

"Gangway! Gangway! Boo! Boo! Boo!" The entire crowd turned to look at Aunt Maggie, riding atop Ebenezum's shoulders as the wizard rushed into our midst. And Maggie was holding Ebenezum's nose!

"Batwom Ignatius, Wuntvor!" my master cried. "Batwom Ignatius!"

"Batwom Ignatius?" I replied.

"Is right!" Death exclaimed. "You've doubled your life! Barring illness or accident, of course."

The crowd started to go wild, but Maggie chanted a few syllables and Ebenezum waved his hands. The crowd noise receded.

Ebenezum sneezed once, loudly, as Aunt Maggie climbed down from his back. I asked him how he knew about Ignatius.

"Had to learn it for my wizard finals," he replied. "It's amazing the useless knowledge they make you pack into your skull."

"Such a pitiful spell," Death remarked. "Why did you do it? They'll all be back in a moment."

"I wanted to talk to you alone," the wizard replied.

"Your affliction will come back, too, when they return. Is that what you're afraid of? Come with me, Ebenezum, and you need never sneeze again."

"Perhaps I will." Ebenezum tugged at his sleeves. "I have heard, Death, that you are fond of games. Will you play one with me?"

Death sneered. "You toy with me, wizard. No one toys with Death! Quick, what will it be? Parcheesi? Contract bridge? Fifty-two pickup?"

The wizard pulled on his beard for a moment, then intoned:

"Arm wrestling."

Death shrugged. "If you insist." He snapped his fingers, and a table and chairs materialized between them.

"Now the terms." Ebenezum looked Death in the eye socket. "If I win, the three of us go free, and Maggie regains her kingdom. If I lose, I am yours."

Death smiled. "For someone of your eminence, anything. I always enjoy welcoming someone whom the bards sing about. After you." He indicated a chair.

Ebenezum sat. I thought that the ghostly crowd noises were somewhat closer. Ebenezum would have to hurry, or his nose might betray him.

Death smoothed his snow-white robe and sat opposite my master. His smile, if anything, was broader than before.

"Shall we begin, dear wizard?"

Ebenezum put his elbow to the table. Death did the same. Their hands clasped.

The ghostly crowd was definitely closer. I could see pale flickerings across the clearing.

"Now!" Death said, and Ebenezum tensed his whole body. There was no movement beyond the constant quiver where the two hands met.

And then the ghosts were back upon us, all talking and screaming and laughing at once. "I'm hit!" "You're out!" "Got you!" "Hot dogs!" "Tickle, tickle, tickle!"

"Dishonest Death!" Maggie screamed. "This was to be an even contest, without your ghostly consorts!"

Death laughed. Maggie said something else that I didn't quite catch.

And Ebenezum sneezed.

And what a sneeze! Ghosts went flying. Death pulled back in alarm and was caught in the gale, along with his table and chair.

It was silent all around. I saw the first light of dawn in the east.

"Will they be back?" I asked, my voice little more than a whisper.

"Alas, Wuntvor," the wizard said, "I fear they haven't the ghost of a chance." Then he blew his nose.

Ebenezum and Maggie walked over to one of the great stones so recently toppled by the wizard's sneezing attack, while I surveyed in wonder the devastation a single great sneeze could bring to this already bleak land. Ebenezum helped Maggie to sit on the fallen boulder, then seated himself.

"How?" was my only question.

"Ebby never could keep a secret from me." Maggie cackled. "But his aversion to sorcery presented something of a problem if we were to survive the night."

My master pulled at his beard. "I freed you from Unwin, remember."

"All I had to do was choose to talk to you rather than him. Unwin always was impossibly jealous. Flew off in an ectoplasmic snit. Which made you sneeze about five times."

Ebenezum tried to say something, but Maggie kept right on talking. "That's when I had the idea. If he always sneezed around the supernatural, what if he really sneezed! We couldn't take away his problem, so the two of us worked up a little spell that would increase Ebby's nasal power a hundredfold!"

"Indeed," Ebenezum said, rubbing his nose, which was red from blowing.

"And now we're safe. And the kingdom is free. Or is it?" Maggie spat on the ground. "Death is such a trickster. I was so afraid of him when Unwin died, I gave in and let him give me five lifetimes for what he termed 'occasional use of my kingdom.' What he didn't tell me was that nothing could live in the kingdom between the times he used it." She looked around her. "Has he kept his word? If only there was a sign."

She slapped Ebenezum's shoulder. "But you still haven't heard my story."

Ebenezum looked out over the hills. "Alas, teacher, we have a long way to travel. Shoulder your pack, Wunt. We'd best move before the sun gets too high."

"You'll sit here and listen!" Maggie commanded. "Ebby never did have any manners. From the beginning. Once there was a beautiful kingdom, and a fair princess. But all was not well, for one day came the dreaded rain of—"

"Ow!" I yelled. Something had bitten my arm.

Ebenezum jumped up. "Biting gnats! They're all over us!"

Maggie threw her hands up to the heavens. "My kingdom is saved!"

"Drop us a note when 'tis a little better developed!" the wizard called over his shoulder.

And we were once again traveling, somewhat more rapidly than before, with frequent slapping of arms and legs, in the general direction of Vushta.

SIX

"A wizard cannot do everything; a fact most magicians are reticent to admit, let alone discuss with prospective clients. Still, the fact remains that there are certain objects, and people, that are, for one reason or another, completely immune to any direct magical spell. It is for this group of beings that the magician learns the subtleties of using indirect spells. It also does no harm, in dealing with these matters, to carry a large club near your person at all times."

—THE TEACHINGS OF EBENEZUM, Volume VIII

My master sneezed at last. I had been expecting it for quite some time. Ever since we had begun our descent into this new valley, three days' distance from our harrowing experience in the Valley of Vrunge, I had once again noticed a general deterioration of the surrounding landscape: a tree uprooted here or there, an occasional house or barn pounded to splinters, whole sections of farmers' fields gouged from the earth. It looked altogether unhealthy.

I think that by this time, neither my master nor myself were particularly surprised by this turn of events. Sorcery seemed to follow us wherever we might go on the trail to Vushta. Still, as Ebenezum had remarked as we sat by our last evening's cookfire, we had not fared badly so far in the midst of all this magic. Indeed, in some cases we had made a fair profit from our sorcerous dealings. In fact, should certain magical events continue to occur on the course of our travels, we might arrive in Vushta as truly wealthy men.

"There is more than one way to look at luck," Ebenezum had concluded as he settled himself down to sleep. "Never look a gift spell in the runes, Wunt."

But that had been easy for the wizard to say the night before, while we were still far away from this present magic. Now, all Ebenezum could do was sneeze.

There was a tremendous crash in the distance. The wizard's sneezes echoed the chaos.

Someone was calling to us. It was a young woman, close to my age. Her long dark hair streamed behind her as she ran in our direction.

"Hide!" she called. "Quickly, hide before Uxtal finds—"She stopped short a few paces from us, a look of consternation on her beautiful face. "You're a wizard!"

Ebenezum stroked his beard and knitted his bushy brows. "How very observant. How may we serve you, my dear?" His sneezing fit seemed to have disappeared behind his veneer of professionalism.

"You can get those robes off as quickly as possible!" Her deep green eyes looked from side to side, taking in all of the valley. "Maybe we can find some old rags to disguise you as a peasant. Does the inlay of silver stars go all the way through to the other side of the fabric? Maybe, if you wore them inside out, we could pretend you were a monk!"

"Young lady!" My master's eyes glowed with sorcerous indignation. "You want me to hide my wizardry?"

"No, no," the woman said impatiently. "'Twould be best to hide if you were just common folk. Being a wizard, 'twould be best if you fled the valley altogether."

It was then that I saw the giant.

The giant roared. He was huge, towering over the tallest trees, his feet spread on either side of a broad, rushing river. His hair was matted, his beard long and unkempt, and he showed uneven, yellowed teeth when he growled. Teeth so large they would have no trouble snapping a person in half.

"Fo fo fum fee," he rumbled. "I don't like these other three." He then tossed a rather large boulder he happened to be holding in our direction.

Ebenezum tried to free his hands from the folds of his robes for a quick conjure, but the presence of the giant threw him into a prolonged sneezing bout before he could even straighten his elbows. I moved toward the young lady, hoping to carry her away from the path of the rapidly descending rock. But she pushed me away.

And said a spell herself.

The boulder flew back toward the giant.

"Fee fo fum fi!" he shrieked. "Time for me to say good-bye!" The giant crashed down into the valley and was soon lost from sight.

I stared at the woman. I realized my mouth was

open. I shut it. So beautiful and so talented! I wondered what it would be like to marry into the profession.

"I saw that!" A small man scurried from behind a ruined stone wall. Ebenezum blew his nose mightily.

The small man hopped across the stony field. He wore some sort of bright-colored uniform, alternately yellow and green, an outfit complemented by the livid red of his complexion.

"You know magic is strictly forbidden!" he shrieked. "Practicing magic means your death!"

The woman looked to where the rock had flown. "It would have meant my death if I had not used magic."

"Technicalities!" the small man screamed. "'Twill not save you from the hangman's noose!" His eyes darted to my master. "You. You're wearing wizard's robes!"

"Indeed. Everyone in your valley is very observant." My master sniffed.

"Well . . ." The man paused, tongue poked in cheek. "You've yet to conjure. With luck, you'll only get twenty years hard labor."

"But they've just entered the valley!" the woman exclaimed. "How could they—"

"Ignorance of the law is no excuse!" The man caught a silver whistle dangling around his neck and blew a mighty blow. "I've called my minions to take you away."

The minions appeared from behind the same stone wall that produced the government official. They were of much the same size as the first man, though of decidedly different origin; mud brown in color, with barbed tails, long taloned arms, and small heads dominated by wide, grinning mouths. They hummed, ominously and in unison.

"Take them to the dungeon in the hill!" The small man managed to shriek and laugh simultaneously.

The dozen minions spread out before us. Their humming grew louder and fiercer as they approached. Ebenezum was lost to us, sneezing somewhere deep within his voluminous robes.

The woman stepped valiantly forward, her hands extended to call magical aid. But would such meager aid as she could summon instantly be enough to defeat a squad of demon-things? Something had to be done.

I stepped to her side and raised my stout oak staff.

"Aha!" the man in uniform cried. "The old man has surrendered, yet you two still resist. Do not cross me!" He, too, waved his hands in front of him in standard conjuring position. "I will show you my power! I warn you, I have been practicing!"

The hands moved through a complicated pattern as the man chanted beneath his breath. He laughed. "See how you contend with this!"

He pointed both his hands at us. For a moment, nothing happened. Then a pair of white birds emerged from his sleeves.

"*I didn't want birds!*" The man's uniform flapped as he jumped up and down. "Minions! Take them away!"

The muddy demons approached. Their humming was all around us. Both the young woman and I took an involuntary step backward and bumped into each other. I turned to stammer an apology, and the demons were upon us.

"Yanna!" she cried. "Nothalatno! Away!"

I struck out with my stout oak staff. My master, attempting to recover and come to our aid, rolled against my foot. From the corner of my eye, I saw a demon grab the woman's hair.

"Look out!" I cried, and swung the staff at the demon without thinking. But the arc of the blow was too great. My feet stumbled against the still sneezing wizard as the staff bounced from the demon's head with a resounding *thwack*!, then ricocheted from the woman's shoulder. She yelped in surprise and fell against me. I completely lost my balance in turn and collapsed atop the stricken mage. Before I could untangle myself, we were all three rolling down the hill.

Ebenezum shouted something as we rolled. When we hit the ground at valley bottom, it felt like a pillow. My master had managed a spell again. At least, I thought it was my master.

"Quick thinking!" the woman said. "My spells were virtually useless. Only brute action of the type you employed could save the day."

"'Twas nothing," I said, humbly studying the rocky ground on which we had landed. "Any magician's apprentice would have done the same."

The young woman mentioned we had not been properly introduced. Her name was Norei.

"Ebenezum," my master said before I could speak. He brushed and straightened his robes. "Mage of the West. My apprentice is Wuntvor."

I bowed slightly and almost fell over. I was, perhaps, still a bit dizzy from our fall. I looked up, and Norei was smiling.

"'Tis fortunate you have come," she said. "We have need of two more heads that are good with spells. My mother, Solima, will be glad for the help. As you see, terrible things are happening in this valley. Things that threaten to destroy not only this community"—she paused, and her voice dropped to a whisper—"but also the very reality in which we live."

What could be so awful as to destroy reality? I looked at my master, but he stared far beyond the hills to either side of us.

"Solima," he whispered.

Norei led us into the woods that seemed to cover much of the valley floor. I followed close at her heels, while Ebenezum trailed some distance behind. She led us down a winding path, well marked in places, overgrown with weeds and brambles in others, until, deep in the forest, we came to a small clearing. A tiny cottage was nestled in one corner of the open space.

"My home," Norei said as she led us through the open door.

"Solima!" my master cried.

A woman of middle years looked up from the pot she was tending and stared at my master. She wiped her hands on her gray robe. "Ebenezum? Is that you?"

"Indeed." My master doffed his wizard's cap. "All the way from the Western Kingdoms. I had heard you might be practicing in the area, but I had little hope of meeting you."

Solima offered my master a sad smile. "It's good to see you, Eb. That white beard fits you; it makes you look less of a scoundrel. Alas, the rest of what you say isn't quite true. Situations have arisen in this valley that may prevent me from ever practicing magic again."

"We met Tork on the way here, Mother."

"So you've met the prince!" Solima pulled a pipe

out of her sleeve and knocked it against the long table that filled the center of the room. "Was he hospitable to the newcomers?"

"He tried to arrest us!" Norei replied.

"For Tork, that's hospitality." She snapped her fingers, and smoke rose from the pipe bowl. She puffed at the stem. "Did you tell them anything of our plight, daughter?"

"I was too worried Tork might find us again."

"Quite so. Let me tell you about our liege lord."

"Solima." Ebenezum took a step forward. "Let me tell you about your eyes."

"Ebenezum! It's been years!" She glared at the wizard with the same green eyes she had given her daughter. "Besides, you're changing the subject. Prince Tork is not a matter to be taken lightly."

My master sighed and shrugged. "Indeed. He was the wizard we met?"

"Well, he fancies himself a wizard. He's never gotten one spell straight that I know of. But he's jealous of all those who can conjure rightly, and so has banned all other wizardry but his throughout the valley."

"He's got everything backward!" Norei added. "His evil spells come out good, and his good spells come out evil!"

"Luckily for us," Solima continued. "Tork's nature is such that he seldom contemplates a good spell. Still, he has managed to conjure all sorts of creatures from the Netherhells, including a giant with a rather foul temper."

Ebenezum scratched at his beard. "It does sound serious. Yet if he is so inept, couldn't you cast a spell to neutralize him or banish him somewhere?"

Solima sighed. "If we had realized in time, it

would have been easy. But Tork is such a buffoon that we ignored him, until suddenly he came marching to our door with an army of demons to take my two sisters captive."

"Blackmailed by an inept wizard . . ." My master's brow furrowed in thought. "There's no way to overcome his allies from the Netherhells?"

"None that I can think of. You know the way my family has always made magic, Ebenezum. 'Tis a collective process, with every woman joining in. That's when our witchery is most powerful. With my two sisters gone, that power is greatly diminished. There's still Norei and Grandmother, of course—"

"Grandmother?" A certain dread had crept into the wizard's voice. "She's still alive?"

Solima nodded. "She lives in the attic."

"Would she remember me?"

"Grandmother forgets nothing."

"Perhaps," Ebenezum said, "my apprentice and I should rest a while. Perhaps in a barn or some outlying field."

"Don't worry. She seldom comes downstairs." Solima banged her pipe against the table again. "Besides, we haven't told you the worst part of Tork's incantations."

Ebenezum glanced at the ladder leading above. "Perhaps if we discussed it while we walked outside? I could stand to stretch my legs."

"Nonsense. Listen to me now. Every time a spell does not work, Tork gets a little more frustrated. And with every frustration, he decides he must tackle a somewhat more complicated spell to prove himself. This disturbing tendency has escalated to such a point that, probably this very night, Tork will attempt Fisbay's Grand Forxsnagel."

What little blood remained in Ebenezum's face vanished entirely. "The Forxsnagel? But should that fail . . ."

"Exactly. I should imagine that this valley would become the eighth Netherhell. And who knows? Perhaps the whole world would follow."

There was silence for a long moment, then Norei spoke. "Perhaps, Mother, the wizard's suggestion is best. We should let the two of them rest. Then, when the Forxsnagel begins, both wizard and apprentice can join us, five strong, to battle it."

Solima puffed on her pipe for a moment, then nodded. Norei led us from the tiny cottage to an even tinier shed in back. Ebenezum followed quietly.

He spoke the instant Norei had left. "She does have the most beautiful green eyes, Wunt. We had our moment together, back when I was near your age. But her grandmother!" He coughed.

I had never seen my master quite like this before. For want of something to say, I asked him about the Forxsnagel.

"Mm?" The question seemed to bring the wizard back to his senses for a moment. "Oh, 'tis the Overspell, the one great conjure that will make the whole world yours for the taking. It's purely theoretical magic, of course, never been attempted before. Ah, but those green eyes, Wunt! I came this way on our journey toward Vushta to see if Solima still lived here. She is a great witch, fully my equal. But when I saw her eyes again, I forgot my malady, the reason, I thought, I had come. Ah, if only the old woman weren't alive!"

I was beginning to seriously worry for my master. His usual professionalism seemed to have vanished with one glance from Solima. He had neglected to tell either of the witches that his ailment prevented him from even being in the presence of wizardry, while I was probably the world's only magician's apprentice who had never been taught any magic. Yet in a matter of hours, we were expected to rally against the greatest spell ever conjured.

An earth tremor shook the shack. There was a giant's foot outside the window.

"Fee fi fo fum! Uxtal for revenge has come!"

The magician held his nose. "'Tis up to us now! Open my pack and get out the red book! Page forty-six!"

I ruffled as rapidly as possible through the jumble of books and arcane equipment. Finally I spied a thin red tome beneath a bundle of dried herbs. I pulled the book from the pack and examined it. *Sorcery Made Simple* was stamped on the cover in large gold letters. Beneath that, in smaller script, were the words "E-Z-Spell Library #6." I rapidly turned to page forty-six as my master finally sneezed.

"THE BANISHMENT OF GIANTS," bold block letters proclaimed across the top. This was followed by a brief description of types of giant—from what little I read, Uxtal seemed to be a Northern Blue—and three short spells for their removal.

That's when Uxtal tore the roof from the shack. Ebenezum's hands flew about his sneeze-racked body, and I found myself encircled by thick gray smoke.

"Fee fi fum fo! Where did those two mortals go?"

I heard Uxtal somewhere above us. Someone grabbed my sleeve and pulled. I stumbled after him.

Then the wizard sneezed again, sending the cloud in all directions.

"Fi fo fum fee! I'll teach you to hide from me!"

The giant reached for us. I still held the red book in my hand but had lost my place. I leafed through frantically, wishing I could remember the page number.

Then I heard the singing. It came from the front doorstep of the cottage, where Norei, Solima, and a wizened old woman I had never seen before stood. It was a strange song, sometimes sounding like a choir of angels had come to earth, other times resembling nothing more than certain yodeling ditties I had been fond of at the age of three. But the song was a spell, and a glowing ball of orange light grew above the three women, then rapidly sped in the direction of the giant. Uxtal turned and ran so fast he didn't have time for parting words.

My master blew his nose.

"You're safe, then!" Norei called. "Would we could get rid of Tork as easily as we subdued Uxtal."

"That the one?" the old woman said as she pointed to Ebenezum. "I remember him! Looks like he's got a cold. He's spreading disease. Mark my word, it wouldn't surprise me if he were carrying the plague!"

"Now, Grandmother," Solima chided.

"He's probably never worked a day of his life! And look at that beard! Norei, get me some eye of newt and toe of frog! We'll teach him to come skulking around here!"

"Grandmother's a traditionalist." Norei leaned close to me and whispered in my ear. My heart raced. "She's never liked wizards much, either. She always thinks they bad-mouth witches."

"Just a second here, and I'll fry up a couple of lightning bolts!" the old woman proclaimed. She rubbed her hands rapidly. "Then I'll zap you back where you came from!"

"Grandmother!" Solima scolded. "You know we can't use magic unless it's absolutely necessary. Tork will find us!"

"This is necessary!" the old woman shouted, her hands still rubbing together. I heard something crackle between them.

"Grandmother! Ebenezum is my friend! I will not have you zapping him!"

"Friend? After what he did to me? I'll show him what I think of his chicken-feather spell!"

"Grandmother! Up to your room!"

The old woman glowered for a moment, then scooted up the ladder. Ebenezum blew his nose.

"You showed great restraint with Grandmother this time, Eb. I do agree that that spell with the chickens was a bit much, especially after all those dead fish. But she was right about your cold, wasn't she?"

Ebenezum looked at me, then at Solima and Norei. His face was drawn and tired. "Alas, 'tis worse than that." And he told them the story of his malady.

"You poor dear!" Solima said when he was through. "You've managed valiantly, though. I always knew you were a man of character, Eb." She walked over to my master and put her hands on his shoulders. "Give me an hour or so to check my books. I'm sure there are certain herbs that can be used to ease a condition such as yours, and if I'm not mistaken, certain healing sprites can be called to visit an area which would remove your condition completely! Face it, you old codger: you haven't been cured because you have not visited a good witch!"

She kissed him on the forehead. "Now I want all three of you out of here. I have to do my research!"

The wizard took me aside as soon as we had quit the cottage. "Vulnerability, Wunt. Always good as a last resort. Brings out the mother instinct. You still have the red book?"

I showed my master where I had tucked it in my shirt.

"Good." He twirled his mustache. "Who knows? Soon I may even be able to use it."

Norei stepped from the door we had just left. "Wuntvor? May I speak to you for a minute?"

I looked to my master. He pulled his beard reflectively.

"Indeed," he said after a moment. "There are matters I must attend to as well." He walked to the remains of the shack, more bounce in his wizardly stride than I had ever seen before.

Then I turned to Norei. My world was Norei—her oval face, framed by long dark hair. And those large green eyes. Eyes to get lost in.

"Wuntvor? What's the matter?" she said with some concern. "Do I have a bug on my nose? You just got the strangest look."

I cleared my throat and stared at the forest floor, assuring her it was only fatigue from my journey.

"Tired you may be, but you have to put that behind you!" She grabbed my arm above the elbow. I looked up. Her face was close to mine. "Your master is ill, my mother close to collapse, Grandmother unwilling to help because of something your master did long ago involving fish and chickens! It's up to the two of us to be strong. We have to be the center around which the magic grows to defeat Tork's Forxsnagel!"

I nodded. Yes, everything she said was true. I would do anything for her. So what if I'd only tried three spells in my life and none of them ever quite worked out? With Norei as my guide, our magic would be strong.

She kissed me lightly. I could hear my brain hum. When she screamed, I realized it wasn't my brain, but the demons. They surrounded us, and their humming was fierce.

"So!" Tork called from the rear of the demon brigade. "Playing with magic this afternoon, were you? I can deal with you now!"

Ebenezum came running from the cottage, followed by Solima. Grandmother hopped quickly behind.

"The only dealing you'll do, fiend," Ebenezum exclaimed, "is with me!"

"Careful, Eb!" Solima cautioned. "I'm not sure of the potency of the herbs. Perhaps we should work our collective magic before they wear off."

"He'll never listen," Grandmother shouted from the rear. "Let the scoundrel go! Give me some foxroot and duckwort, and I'll show them all!"

In the midst of this, Tork tried to conjure. Frogs fell from his sleeves.

"No! No!" he screamed. "Very well! You've sealed your doom! The Overspell! *Forxsnagel!*"

The earth shook.

"Fee fi fo fum! I will stamp on everyone!"

Uxtal was above us. Norei ran to her family. The three of them began a chant. Glancing back, Ebenezum joined in as Prince Tork screamed incantations and jumped through a series of extremely acrobatic positions.

"Fi fo fum fee! No one's even watching me!" The

giant growled and lifted his great foot into the air.

I looked back and forth at the two groups of combatants: leaping Tork surrounded by demons, the three witches and Ebenezum weaving a vocal tapestry. Uxtal, I reasoned, would stomp the singers first, but the four were so involved in their song they would never see the descending foot.

'Twas then I remembered the book. I pulled it all too rapidly from my shirt. It spun from my hands and landed on the ground. When I picked it up, I noticed it had opened to the proper page!

I knew then that I was fated to best the giant. I glanced rapidly over the three spells printed across the bottom of the page. I chose what appeared to be the simplest: "Shrinking the Giant Down to Size." A six-foot-tall giant would be no problem at all!

But I had forgotten the demons! They were all upon me, ripping and tearing at my clothes, their awful hum close against my ears. I shouted out the spell, the book ripped from my hands as the final syllables escaped my lips.

The demons fell away from me. I looked up to the giant. He was getting smaller!

But my exhilaration was short-lived. For some reason, everything else was getting smaller, too.

I realized my mistake. In my haste, I must have jumbled the syllables of the spell. Instead of Uxtal shrinking, I was growing!

I looked about me as I grew to Uxtal's size and more. It gave me a whole new view of the countryside; the ruined half of the valley where we had descended, and the area around me, which, besides a few spots like the demolished shack, seemed still to be the rolling forest and picturesque farmland this whole valley must have been before the coming of Uxtal.

I noticed then that my stout oak staff had grown with me. Far below, I could hear Prince Tork's screams, counterpointed by four voices weaving in and out, punctuated by shrill whistles and wild whoops. None of them seemed in the least aware of the giant's foot hovering over them.

"Fee fum fo fi! I will crush you by and by!"

I hit his foot with my staff. Uxtal looked up in alarm.

"Hey!" he said in a low voice. "You trying to spoil my act?"

"Away, fiend!" I bellowed. I was surprised at how loud my voice was.

"Away, fiend? What kind of line is that? It doesn't even rhyme! I was only trying to scare the folks. It's part of the contract!"

"A contract with demons!" I cried. I walked toward Uxtal. Things crunched and crashed beneath my feet. I looked down to see my gigantic boots had left a trail of decimation through the forest.

"Say," Uxtal said, his eyes narrowed to slits, "are you nonunion?"

He was trying to confound me with Netherhell double-talk! I decided, rather than risk destroying more of the valley bottom, I would stand my ground and thrash the villain soundly with my staff. I swung the stick with a cry.

And Uxtal jumped out of its path. He was awfully limber for a giant. The staff swept empty air, and I lost my balance. I found myself falling, straight toward Ebenezum and the witches.

Frantically, I tried to twist away. I crashed, scant

yards away from the whooping and whistling assembly, demolishing the witches' cottage instead.

I rolled away from the witches' clearing, flattening another couple of acres of forest, and struggled to my feet. Now I was mad! I growled at Uxtal.

"You had better get out of here!"

Uxtal was looking down at the others. A great ball of light had formed above the witches, while Tork had created a large area of total dark above himself. Light and dark moved together.

"I think you're right." Uxtal waved and in four strides had disappeared over the rim of the valley.

Dark and light met.

It turned very cold, and all the color seemed to drain from the world. There was no sound; only gray shapes in silence. I could see the four still singing, and Tork dancing among his demons.

But something was wrong with Ebenezum! He was down on his knees. Even though there was no sound, I knew he was sneezing.

The world was going a deeper gray. Ebenezum tried to rise but fell, quivering in his robes. I tried to move, to help my master, but was somehow glued to the spot.

The world went dark.

In an instant, there was light. The three witches lay on the ground, unconscious. Ebenezum had somehow managed to stand, and now faced Tork and his demon minions, who all hummed triumphantly.

"The Forxsnagel is mine!" Tork cried. "I can have anything I want! Already I have defeated the power of these three witches. You ceased your spells just before the blow and were spared. But that, dear wizard, is a temporary condition! By the power of the Forxsnagel, I claim your wizard's skills!"

Dark lightning flashed from Tork's fingers. Ebenezum threw out his hands to conjure himself, but the lightning threw him back.

Tork laughed, raising his balled fist to the heavens. "Power! All of magic is mine!"

Then he began to sneeze.

Norei and I kissed. A young witch and a magician's apprentice, in a world made new again.

The witches had managed to return the valley to normal in a surprisingly short time. Solima's sisters were rescued from their prison, the demons exorcised from the land, and rebuilding had begun. My master and I should have left a week before to continue our journey to Vushta, city of a thousand forbidden delights and a cure for my master. But here we stayed. Which was fine with me.

I kissed Norei. Her lips were very sweet.

It was a shame about Ebenezum's cure, though. When Tork had achieved Forxsnagel, he had tried to drain off my master's abilities and received Ebenezum's malady in the bargain. Now Solima was afraid to summon such sprites as might cure my master, in case they cured Prince Tork as well. There were still the herbs, of course, though Solima warned against using them too frequently. They had taken their toll on Ebenezum already; he had slept for most of a day after his battle with Tork. And Solima told us that after two or three ingestions, the body built up immunities to the medicine, and the malady would return, as bad as or worse than ever. We would have to go to Vushta after all.

Norei's cool hand brushed the hair from my eyes. "What are you thinking of, Wunt?"

"Fate," I replied. "How we met, and suffered, and triumphed. How we both have our whole lives ahead of us, and how my future has changed, knowing you."

Norei's green eyes looked heavenward. "You do talk funny sometimes, Wuntvor. We've just met. Don't go planning our lives yet. Who knows what will happen to us?" She kissed my cheek.

"Who knows?" I agreed. "For now, my master seems content to stay here." I looked back at the rebuilt cottage, half-hidden by what trees still remained standing in this part of the wood.

There was a rumbling crash.

"Ha, ha, ha! I knew the duckwort would work!" It was Grandmother's voice. "I'll teach you to lay about the house sweet-talking my daughter!"

Ebenezum came running full speed from the cottage. Solima held her grandmother back from following. Fire sprouted from the old woman's fingertips.

"The spells may take a little while, but the old ways are the best!" the old woman called. "Stand your ground and let me boil your blood!"

My master tossed me my pack. "Quick, Wunt! It's off to Vushta!" He sneezed and looked back at Solima. "I'll be back when I've found the cure!"

"I look forward to it!" Solima replied, still grasping the struggling oldster.

"We'll all be waiting for you!" Grandmother waved her flaming hands.

I stood, pack in one hand, staff in the other. "I guess I'm off to Vushta, then."

"Oh," Norei replied. "Well, good-bye."

Is that all she had to say? After all the time we

spent together? "Norei," I whispered, "come to Vushta."

She looked at me and smiled.

"They call it the city of a thousand forbidden delights."

"Well, maybe I will, someday." She stood and kissed me lightly.

"Now I'll zap you, scoundrel!" Grandmother had broken free from Solima and was coming toward us rapidly. Her fire fingers singed the shrubbery as she ran. "I'll teach you to sully the name of good, honest witches! Fish and chickens, indeed!"

I was off down the road, after my master.

"No matter how ideal the circumstances of one's present location," he remarked as I caught up with him, "there is always something to be said for a change of scene."

SEVEN

"There are those who claim that magic is like the tide; that it swells and fades over the surface of the earth, collecting in concentrated pools here and there, almost disappearing from other spots, leaving them parched for wonder. There are also those who believe that if you stick your fingers up your nose and blow, it will increase your intelligence."

—THE TEACHINGS OF EBENEZUM, Volume VII

After that, of course, our luck got worse. It wasn't just the assassins, although Urfoo's paid minions kept appearing with greater and greater frequency. It was probably all those minstrels that made us so easy to find. When one's fame is being sung in every village in the kingdom, it is difficult for one to travel incognito. Before our present arrangement, we seemed to be always on the run.

Then the earthquakes began.

At first, they were only small tremors, a moment's

shifting of the earth beneath our feet. But they grew greater day by day. I worried that Prince Tork had recovered from his inherited malady and would soon visit the Forxsnagel upon us again. When I told my master of my fears, he dismissed them, at least as far as so inept as wizard as Tork was concerned. Yet as to the earthquakes being caused by the Forxsnagel . . . well, there might be some truth to that. He would speak no more on the subject until we were free of our present company. Until then, he only scratched the hair beneath his cap.

Our conversation was cut short by a commotion in the distance.

There must have been twenty of them, each one attempting to scream louder than his or her companions, all running full tilt down the dirt path that passed for a road in this rural clime. On my master's instructions, we stepped to one side of the lane and watched them pass.

"Indeed," Ebenezum intoned as the cloud of dust caused by the commotion settled down again upon the road. He allowed a hand to stroke his beard and made clicking sounds deep in his throat, a sure sign of wizardly thought.

"I do believe they would have run us over!" Old Dame Sniggett quivered, her pale hands fluttering amongst her black robes. "They can't be from around here! Not civilized at all!"

"Now, now, Auntie." The beautiful Ferona took her elder's hands in her own steady grip. In the two days that the women had been our traveling companions, I had been repeatedly impressed by the young woman's ability to remain calm in the face of any crisis.

"I'm sure there is some logical explanation for

their behavior," she continued. "Perhaps they are some sort of religious order, making a hasty pilgrimage to their holy shrine. Whatever their purpose, it is not for us to worry about. Not when we are so close to the safety of our home."

The wizard turned to regard the two women. "We are almost there?"

Ferona smiled, an expression so brilliant on her freckled face, surrounded by her red hair, that if you watched her long enough, you might forget the sun. "Aye, good sir. We are nearly in shouting distance. 'Tis only a couple more hills down the road. Come on, Nanny. Let's all of us walk so we can get home and rest properly."

It was then my master sneezed. I hoped, for a foolish instant, that it was only a reaction to the dust on the road. But I knew, somewhat closer to my soul, that my master's sneeze boded far more ill than that.

The wizard sneezed again. A lone man ran toward us this time, his shadow flung far across the road by the late afternoon sun.

"The sun is setting!" the newcomer cried, his voice cracking from the weight of emotion. "The sun is setting!"

"We thank you for that information," my master replied when it became apparent the man had finished his speech. "Is there anything else you'd like to add?"

"But—" The man came closer still. I could now see the horror in his eyes. "'Tis the first night of the full moon!"

The wizard scratched at the snow-white hair beneath his cap. "This is also true." He glanced at the ladies. "If you have no more information to impart, I think we should be on our way."

"Bork, you are talking nonsense!" Dame Sniggett stepped forward. "Pardon the intrusion, oh learned sir, but I know this man. He's one of my farm hands. I almost didn't recognize him, acting so." She sniffed. "He's usually so civilized."

"Oh, my lady!" Bork fell to his knees. "I'm so afraid of the beast, I didn't see you. So much has happened at the farm since the change came over Greta."

The elder pulled herself erect, her once watery eyes afire with outrage. "Something has happened to Greta?"

"No, nothing," Bork whimpered. "That is, nothing beyond . . ." He glanced at my master and myself, and his voice trailed off to nothing.

Ferona looked to Ebenezum, an apologetic smile lighting her face. If only she would smile that way at me! "Greta is my mistress's prize pullet."

My master pulled at his beard. "There is an illness among the chickens, then?"

"Chickens?" Dame Sniggett's voice reached a volume and timbre that I previously would have thought impossible in a woman so frail. "Greta is no—" Her mouth refused to form the word. "Greta is an East Kingdom dandy!"

"Mistress!" Ferona urged. "Your nerves!"

Dame Sniggett glanced, startled, at her young charge. The air seeped from her body in a rush, and she returned to being bent and frail. "Forgive me, good sir," she whispered to my master. "When I hear my Greta is in trouble, all sense leaves me."

"No need for alarm, dear woman," Ebenezum said with the same warm smile and soothing voice that had won a thousand paying clients. "We all have those things that are very dear to us."

The woman glanced at him and quickly looked away. She giggled, a most unexpected sound. "We are fortunate," she said softly, "to be traveling with a man who knows the proper manner in which to view things."

"It's a wizard's duty to place things in perspective. My lady, if you and your ward will accompany me, we will escort you to the safety of your home." With that, Ebenezum led the way down the road once again. I took up the rear as usual, the paraphernalia-filled pack on my back somewhat hindering my movements. Bork struggled to his feet as I passed.

"But the beast—" he cried.

Somewhere in the distance, a wolf howled.

The pounding started sometime after they deposited my master and myself in the massive front hall of the estate. Occasionally, the pounding would be accompanied by screaming.

Dame Sniggett would flutter through the hall from time to time, fragments of explanation trailing her rapid movements. "The rooms aren't quite proper yet. . . . I like everything *just* so. . . . It was so much more civilized." Ferona would glide after her every now and then, and spare a smile for my master. I tried to get her to smile at me but once again couldn't quite catch her eye.

No one mentioned the pounding and the screams.

Both seemed to come from just the other side of the great oak door that formed the entrance way to the massive estate that housed Dame Sniggett and Ferona. In a quiet moment, I asked the wizard what he thought all the commotion might be. My master thought for a bit, then replied in a low tone: "The rich do have their quirks. Most likely 'tis a deranged uncle they keep locked in the tower. Pretend not to notice, at least until they've given us dinner."

At last a young woman appeared to tell us we could now enter the main hall and all would be explained. She introduced herself as Borka, sister to the mistress's other servant. My master turned from his study of the elaborate carvings that lined the walls, especially those inlaid with gold, and pulled at his robes to properly straighten the lines. I gathered up my pack and stout oak walking staff, and followed the wizard into the Great Hall.

Our eyes immediately fixed upon the dozen golden chicken coops that lined one wall of the huge room.

"Welcome to my little nest," Dame Sniggett cooed.

She stood at the end of a long table made of dark wood, Ferona at her side. They had changed from their simple but elegant traveling clothes to somewhat more resplendent finery, the mistress of the house dressed all in black lace, her lovely charge dressed in a gown that showed all the colors of spring. This time I thought Ferona smiled at both of us. I wished again I could get her to smile just for me.

My life had changed in the two days since we had chanced to meet the two women in a roadside inn. Praise the assassins that Urfoo sent against us, for they made it necessary for us to find traveling companions! And thus far, it had worked. The last two days had passed assassin free. But far more than that had happened to me. Before, I had been merely Wuntvor, a magician's apprentice content with following my master on his quest for a cure. But on that day when Dame Sniggett had requested the wizard's aid, my life had grown to include Ferona. There had been a few other women, surely, but their memories were like wisps of smoke, burned away by Ferona's fiery beauty. Well . . . there were some times, late at night, when I thought of Norei, and the way she kissed. But she had her own life to lead. That was something she had made very clear. After that, I shouldn't have thought about her as much as I did. But then there was Ferona!

Ferona! How had I existed before I had known that name? I hadn't yet been able to get her to talk to me, but that was a small matter, now that we had met. Now, my life had purpose.

A chicken clucked. It was probably in response to the immense quantity of pounding and screaming still going on outside, so loud now we could hear it clearly in this inner room.

"Now, now, Greta," Dame Sniggett soothed. "I want you to meet a very important man." Her watery eyes blinked at my master. "Tall, handsome, and a wizard besides!"

"Indeed," Ebenezum rumbled. He glanced briefly at me before returning to examine the hen. I could tell immediately that he was not pleased at being introduced to a chicken. Even with all her money, Dame Sniggett might go too far.

"Borka. Take Greta from her cage."

The wizard grimaced. He expected the worst. He might even have to hold it.

"Yes, ma'am." The serving woman curtsied and grabbed the chicken by the throat.

"Gently, gently," the dame chided. "She is very special to me." I could see the idea of being chased by assassins appealed more to Ebenezum with every passing moment.

"You see, Greta is a very special chicken." Dame

Sniggett's voice fell to a whisper. "She has the ability to produce gold."

The smile reappeared on Ebenezum's lips, unfolding like a flower as it catches the warm rays of the sun.

"It's always been possible in theory," the wizard remarked, "though I've never seen a spell that made it happen. She actually produces golden eggs?"

There was an embarrassed silence. Finally, Borka cleared her throat. "Well, you see, the gold really comes out of another part of the chicken entirely."

"How improper!" Fire blazed in the mistress's eyes again, but the look softened as she gazed at her hen. "Yet poor Greta can't help it. All the creatures of the world must perform such functions, even humans. Cursed with such a fate, we should be thankful when it comes out gold!"

Borka looked up from where she held the chicken. Her face grew suddenly pale. "'Tis getting dark. I must go close the shutters!"

She thrust the chicken back into its cage and ran from the room. The pounding outside seemed to redouble with the approaching darkness, although by now the screams had gotten quite hoarse.

"Now that you know about our Greta," Dame Sniggett said, "I can tell you the real reason I've asked you to come to the estate. When I saw you were a wizard, new hope rose within my bosom. Tell me, dear, dear Ebenezum, might there be a spell by which you could change the orifice through which Greta's gold appears?"

"An interesting point." Ebenezum sniffed. Being in the same room as an enchanted chicken did not seem to be enough to make my master sneeze, although it did make his nose run. I imagined that if

Greta decided to make gold any time in the wizard's presence, his malady would return full force. "Many magicians have proposed spells for the laying of golden eggs," he continued, "but no matter what the process proposed, the results always proved to be economically unfeasible. That is, more magic went in one end than gold came out the other." Ebenezum blew his nose.

"But it might be done?"

"Certainly possible, with the head start your hen has. It's just a matter of fathoming the proper spell of transference."

"Then I must insist you remain here as my guests!" Dame Sniggett's watery eyes shone like pools beneath the moon. "Ferona will show you to your room, civilized in every respect! It belonged to the master of the house, Ferona's late uncle. Oh, and your apprentice can sleep in the barn."

A sudden commotion seemed to have replaced the pounding and screaming that went on in the hallway. Bork staggered into the room.

"Why didn't you answer the door? The beast would have gotten me!"

Dame Sniggett stared at him in silent indignation.

"How were we to know you would return?" Ferona replied. "We thought the knocking was yet another pilgrim, looking for a handout for his holy cause." She glanced at Ebenezum and myself. "All the pilgrims around here know that Auntie has money."

A sudden chill wind blew into the room. Bork, Ferona, and Dame Snigget looked at one another, an expression of terror on their faces.

"The door!" Bork whispered.

Something leapt into the room with a horrible,

shrieking growl. Dame Sniggett cried out, Ferona and Bork leapt away.

Ebenezum was sneezing now. The creature was sorcerous! Although one look at the thing's near human height, its face full of fangs and coarse gray hair, should have been enough to tell me that. The things would kill us all, unless someone acted quickly. I leapt forward, swinging my stout oak staff.

The creature grabbed the swinging wood and wrenched it from my grasp as if the force behind my blow had been nothing. Talons bit into the skin of my right hand. With a cry I pulled myself free, but the creature was on top of me. It forced me to the floor, its breath hot on my neck. I caught a glimpse of razor teeth. Behind us, the chickens shrieked in dismay.

The beast paused and looked up, sniffing the air. As fast as it had floored me, it leapt away to grab the nearest chicken. Hen in mouth, it ran from the room.

As I stared dumbly at my bleeding hand, I heard Ebenezum blow his nose. Dame Sniggett tossed a napkin in my direction so that I might mop up the blood, her face a mask of distaste. Ferona sighed and shook her head.

"It happens all the time."

EIGHT

*"Even for a wizard there will often come
times when someone close to you, perhaps even
your spouse, criticizes your habits by comparing
them to those of animals. This is distinctly un-
fair to the animals, who have far better habits
than we in many areas. When, for example, have
you seen a frog collecting taxes or a squirrel running for electoral office? Present arguments like
these to those people who criticize you. If they
still do not see the wisdom of your ways, you
may then feel free to bite them."*

—THE TEACHINGS OF EBENEZUM, Volume IX

"There are certain problems with this estate," Dame
Sniggett admitted after we had eaten and she had suf-
ficiently calmed.

"Indeed. Like werewolves." Ebenezum stroked
his beard. So that was what it was! I had heard of
such strange creatures—humans that turn to animals

131

under the full moon. My hand ached in remembrance.

"No," Ferona interjected. "What Auntie is trying to say is that magic collects here, producing all manner of strange and wonderful things. Only in such a place could Greta produce gold. Unfortunately, there are negative sides to the magic as well."

"Yes, yes, but that's why we've brought a wizard here!" The aunt smiled at my master. "Good Ebenezum, surely you can try to dispel the negative magicks that lurk about this farm."

"I can but try," the wizard replied. Apparently, no one had noticed my master's total helplessness during the werewolf's attack, and the mage, sensing a fee, was not eager to bring the matter up. "Now, we have had a long and trying day. Perhaps you would be good enough to show us to our rooms?"

"Certainly. Ferona, take Ebenezum up to the master's suite. After that, Bork can point out the way for Wuntvor to walk to the barn." Dame Sniggett studied her black lace sleeve for an instant. "Oh, incidentally, good wizard, just so there are no more surprises, I should tell you to totally ignore the ghost. He's quite harmless, really."

"Ghost?" I saw my master's eyes cloud with wizardly rage. Dame Sniggett had gone too far at last. His right hand shot out to pave the way for a major denunciation. His fingers banged into the golden chicken cage.

The wizard hesitated, the touch of precious metal bringing him back to his senses.

"Beg pardon, madam, but I cannot sleep with a ghost present. My magical senses are too finely tuned; I would get no rest at all. Give my apprentice the master's quarters. I shall sleep in the barn."

Dame Sniggett frowned. "That's hardly proper! Still, who am I to criticize the methods of a practicing wizard? I'm sure, in time, we'll all be able to make the necessary adjustments." She waved her hand. "Bork, show the young man the way upstairs."

Somewhat dejectedly, I followed the servant. I had hoped that Ferona would escort me. I stumbled into the huge bedroom Bork led me to and fell upon the massive bed. My recent fight had exhausted me. Bork departed, closing the door after him. The room was left in darkness.

"Hey," a voice whispered in my ear. "Hey, buddy."

My mind floundered on the edge of sleep. "Wha?"

Encouraged, the voice got louder. "Hey, buddy, ever hear the one about the farmer's daughter and the traveling tinsmith?"

"What?" I was wide awake now. "What are you talking about?"

"All right, all right, so you've heard that one," the voice said, suddenly defensive. "How about this: How many monks does it take to empty a cistern?"

"I was trying to sleep!" I cried. It then occurred to me that I had no idea who or what I was talking to. Ice rolled down my spine. A valley full of ghosts came to mind, a valley where I had almost become a ghost myself.

"Who are you?" I whispered.

"Oh, I'm a ghost. Peelo's the name. Formerly jester to the court of King Zingwarfel, some four hundred years back now. I had the misfortune to make a joke about the king's name, and was put instantly to death. Now I'm forced to wander these halls endlessly, trying to make people laugh. But hey, you don't want to hear about this. It's showtime!"

I had no idea what this creature was talking about. It didn't seem dangerous, but with ghosts you could never tell. "Why can't I see you?" I asked.

"What, you want me to manifest myself? I usually save that for the big boffo conclusion. But hey. Tell me this. Why did the hippogriff cross the road?"

"I don't care!" I pounded the bed with my fists. The right one throbbed painfully. "Ghosts, werewolves, magic chickens. What's going on here?"

"Hey, buddy, calm down. It's all just part of the package. You know, standard Netherhell grab bag: one gold-producing spell, a werestone, a giant Grak—although heaven knows where it's gone—one slightly used ghost. I'm sort of the M.C. of this troupe, forced to walk these halls until I can make someone really laugh. If only somebody would give me some new jokes! Do you know how difficult it is to milk laughs out of four-hundred-year-old material?"

"I'm sure it's hard," I said. I was too tired to care. I lay back on the bed.

"But hey, no more boring stories! On with the show! Did you hear the one about the unicorn and the tavern keeper? Well, this unicorn goes into this tavern, see, and orders a mug of ale from the tavern keeper. The tavern keeper brings the ale, and says, 'That'll be a hundred gold crowns.' Then he adds, 'You know, we don't get many . . .' "

It was all too much for me. I fell asleep.

I found my way to the barn and told Ebenezum my ghost story early the next morning.

"Indeed," he said when I was finished. "There's

more here than meets either the eye or nose. I have a feeling that Dame Sniggett is attempting to extract a great deal of work from us for a very low fee." He cleared his throat. "I imagine she would think that sort of thing proper."

"Either that," I added, "or she's afraid a spell that took away the bad might take her beloved chicken, too."

"A good point." Ebenezum fingered his long white mustache. "Perhaps there's hope for you, yet, Wuntvor. Whatever happens, we'll have to charge for the spells as piecework. Expensive that way, but they can afford it."

"But—" A sudden awkwardness kept me from finishing the sentence. Who was going to cast the spells? My master's malady left him in no condition to conjure. He had tried innumerable methods of blocking up his nose or somehow diverting the sorcerous smells during the course of our travels. The only common element in all these methods was that none of them worked. None of them, that is, except one. Solima's cure!

My eyes wandered to the vial of herbs Ebenezum had kept by his side this past week. The wizard shook his head. "No, Wunt. This job is nowhere near important enough for me to use my only remedy. It will have to wait for a more serious occasion."

Ebenezum pulled at his beard and stared off into the hayloft. "There are a number of supernatural factors at work here. Yet each one, taken separately, is manageable with a fairly simple spell. A werestone must be destroyed, a ghost banished, perhaps another thing or two exorcised. After that, we'll repair Dame Sniggett's chicken. And you, Wuntvor, will be the one to perform the magic."

I stared at my master for a long moment. "Close your mouth, lad. A good wizard always has his mouth firmly closed."

I complied.

"In the past," my master continued, "you have learned to use some simple spells to extricate us from difficult circumstances. Perhaps they haven't always worked exactly as planned, but we are still alive and on the road to Vushta, which is all that really matters. In the next few hours, you will learn a group of spells so simple as to be child's play. After that, all that will be required is the proper timing."

I was overwhelmed. Never had my master placed such faith in me!

"I hope I will be worthy."

Ebenezum raised one eyebrow. "So do I. There's a large fee involved."

When Ferona came to the door of the barn, I hardly looked at her. My head was filled with General Banishment Spell #3, Ork's Rule of Universal Exorcism, and The Great Foudou's Chant for the Realignment of Bodily Parts.

"Excuse me," she said. "Is Ebenezum about?"

She had spoken to me! All the spells flew from my head. At last, what I had dreamed of for so long had come to pass. I searched my thoughts to come up with a reply worthy of her beauty.

But there was no reply that magnificent. I told her, therefore, that Ebenezum had gone out for a walk about the estate.

"A pity," she replied. "Tell me, Wuntvor, what do you think of marriage?"

What was she saying? I had known, deep in my

heart, that once Ferona and I spoke, everything would change. But this quickly?

"It can be a good thing," I prompted.

Ferona nodded absently. "Do you think Ebenezum would consider marrying a woman as young as I?"

I found myself at a loss for words.

"Please close your mouth, Wuntvor," Ferona said. "There are flies in the barn. It could be unhealthy." One of her magnificently formed feet scuffed at a small pile of hay. "You're surprised I want to marry a wizard. It's just that there's such a concentration of magic around here that we'd all feel more secure with a magician about."

I couldn't help myself then. My emotions had risen above reason. "What about me?" I blurted. "I'm a magician, too. Much closer to your age."

"And much less experienced than your master." Ferona frowned. "Let me tell you, Wuntvor, there is another reason that I need an older wizard. There is a curse upon me. Any man under the age of thirty that I kiss dies in three hours!"

I took a step backward.

"I used to have a dozen suitors knocking on my door day and night. It was only after the third one expired that I realized the true horror of my affliction."

"What happened to the other nine?" I asked weakly.

"Oh, they all became pilgrims. I'm afraid there aren't many job opportunities for young men in the Eastern Kingdoms these days. Fortunately, there always seem to be some openings in being holy." She sighed wistfully. "If only one of them were kissing me now!"

I thought for one wild moment about taking their place, but then I remembered the curse. I'd have to learn a spell to lift that as well.

"A curse, too?" Ebenezum had come to stand in the door as we spoke. "Young woman, I think you need to explain the entire situation."

And Ferona told the story of how her uncle thought himself a clever businessman and made a deal with the Netherhells for what seemed to be a limitless supply of gold. But, as is almost always the case in such dealings, he had missed the small print (it is usually so small that people mistake it for a dust mote in the lower left corner of the contract) and, besides a gold-producing chicken, received a ghost, a curse upon his niece, a stone that regularly turned one member of the household into a werewolf, and a large, dark bird that immediately carried Uncle away.

"As you can imagine, we were a little upset over this turn of events," Ferona continued. "However, Auntie insisted that there was a proper way out of this dilemma. All we had to do was bring in an expert in the field, and until then, leave things pretty much the way they were at Uncle's hasty departure, in case he should suddenly return."

"Indeed," Ebenezum replied. "That way you might be able to keep the magic elements from unsettling even further. And do you have a copy of this contract?"

"Alas, no. It was carried away with Uncle when the creature got him."

"A typical Netherhell ploy!" Ebenezum strode back and forth between the haystacks. "Well, we can't face the ghost until nightfall, nor will we see the werewolf. The werestone is another matter entirely.

We must find where the demons put it!"

"Oh!" Ferona said brightly. "The demons put it on a mantelpiece in the Great Hall."

The wizard stared at the young woman. "And you've done nothing with it?"

"Well, Auntie's afraid to move anything in case Uncle won't recognize the place when he returns. Besides which, if you don't bother the werewolf when it bursts into the room, all it does is steal a chicken and run away again."

"Don't you fear for Greta?"

"A little, but so far the werewolf grabs one of the chickens at either end. As long as we keep the prize hen toward the middle, she seems to be fine."

Ebenezum frowned at the fading light outside the barn. My instruction in magic had taken most of the day.

"If we don't hurry," the mage said, "we will be face to face with the werewolf all over again. We'll destroy the werestone now. My assistant, incidentally, will do the actual work while I supervise. Wuntvor needs the practice."

"All right." Ferona looked doubtful. "But we should hurry. The last person the werewolf caught playing with the werestone got his throat torn out."

I swallowed hard and followed my master toward the house. I repeated the three spells, a word for every step I took. There could be no mistakes this time. I had to remember every one, or I would be minus a throat.

"You're sure nothing will happen to Greta?" Dame Sniggett cooed in the direction of her prize hen. The chicken, for its part, ignored the people in the room entirely, pecking away at a pile of dried corn.

"Reasonably sure," the wizard replied. "It depends on the degree of interconnection between the different spells from the Netherhells. Rest assured we will take every precaution."

Ebenezum held his nose. "Wuntvor, open the box."

I did as I was told. A small green stone lay in the middle of the box's plush purple interior. It looked harmless enough. One could hardly imagine it was capable of doing the things Ebenezum had described earlier in the day.

"The werestone," my master explained, "is a particularly fiendish invention of the Netherhells. It causes people who touch it to be driven out into the wilds in the full moon, and the first lower animal they contact, they become like that animal every time the full moon returns. One imagines this particular stone had an additional curse on it, so that the first person to come in contact with it would be forced to seek out a wolf. Otherwise, the person would just have likely turned into a wererabbit."

Ebenezum sneezed behind me. "The spell!" he called. "The spell, Wuntvor!"

I began to recite the neutralizing spell. Somebody screamed when I was halfway through.

"Hey, folks!" an all-too-familiar voice cried out behind me. "It's showtime! Tell me, how many Vushtans does it take to do something forbidden?" I could see a pale jester's scepter out of the corner of my eye. Peelo seemed to have manifested himself for the occasion.

I tried to push the ghost's bad jokes out of my mind. I had to finish the spell! Ebenezum was sneezing with a vengeance now. His nasal whoops threatened to drown out an interminable story on the ghost's part concerning two hairy dogs and a large quantity of mulled wine.

"They're interconnected!" my master managed between sneezes. "Try the"—sneeze—"strongest"—sneeze— "Banish! Banish!"

So I was to go all out! The banishment spell it would be, then. I carefully phrased the first line, making sure I hit all the guttural stops.

That's when I heard the growl behind me.

I leapt to one side as the werewolf lunged and heard cloth tear as the claws grazed my leggings. The creature would kill me now. I needed a weapon.

My stout oak staff was still across the room, near the spot where I had jumped away. The wolf circled the room, running perilously close to the golden chicken coops and the huddled forms of Dame Sniggett and Ferona. Would the beast devour Greta as well? If only there was something to stab, to hit, to throw. Ebenezum could be of no help now. The appearance of the wolf had made his condition even worse. He lay on the floor, a pitiful mass of sneezing flesh.

I had to get my staff! I took a step across the room, but the wolf was in front of me, its fangs bared in a half-human smile. It was stalking me now.

I would have to use my hands. There was nothing else to defend myself with. Then my eye caught the werestone.

In a single motion, I grabbed the thing and flung it at the wolf. It bounced off the creature's head, throwing it off-balance. Stone and wolf both fell against the huddled women.

I hadn't meant to do that. I started across the room in an attempt to rescue someone, when I saw the stone take its effect on the other two. Both Ferona and Dame Sniggett had grown dark, coarse hair all over their bodies. Where once there was one werewolf, now there were three.

Still, I would continue to fight! Though the odds were great against me, I would give my last ounce of blood to protect my master. Let the werewolves do their worst!

It occurred to me then that I had also touched the werestone. Should a werewolf touch me now, I would also turn into a hairy beast. There'd be no hope for Ebenezum then. The wolves, myself included, would tear him apart.

The creatures were on Ebenezum! The wizard flailed at them with his fists, but he could barely control his movements. A small vial fell from among his robes. The herbal remedy!

I dove beneath a clawed hand and tossed the vial back to my master. My momentum carried me on headfirst into the golden chicken cages.

I felt the change come over me then. My nose and mouth grew together and became hard. I felt my arms sprout feathers. I knew then the horrible truth. I was turning into a werechicken!

A wolf sprang at me, and I pecked it savagely with my beak. Startled, the wolf backed away. It had obviously never dealt with a six-foot chicken before. Surprise was on my side for a moment. But once the wolves regrouped, their teeth and claws would tear me apart in an instant.

My chicken eyes saw movement. Ebenezum placed the vial to his lips and swallowed.

There was a crash of breaking glass, and a great, dark bird entered the room. "Ladies and gentlemen!" Peelo the ghost cried. "The return of the Grak!"

I saw then that the Grak was carrying a small, balding gentleman. "Home at last!" the balding man cried.

The wolves rushed me. Ebenezum was on his feet, conjuring mightily. As they ran, the wolves transformed to Borka, Ferona, and Dame Sniggett.

The bird circled overhead. It was too much for my master, even with the medicine. He collapsed again, sneezing.

"Feerie!" cried the man dangling from the dark bird's claws. "Borkie! Sniggie! How good to see you again! I thought I'd never escape the Netherhells. They have awful, torturous things there. Traffic jams! Aspirin commercials!"

But even the uncle's babbling could not deter Peelo. His four hundred-year-old material just kept on coming.

"Ladies and gentlemen!" he cried, pointing at me. "A practical demonstration! Why did the chicken cross the moat?"

Ferona took one look at me and laughed. I clucked in indignation. Didn't she realize who helped save her?

"A laugh," Peelo whispered. "An honest laugh. We're free to leave this dull estate! Back to the excitement of the Netherhells. I tell you, the old jokes are always the best!"

With that, the ghost disappeared. As did all other things supernatural.

The long silence was broken by Greta's frantic clucking. I turned to look at the chicken and noticed that the feathers had left my arms. Seeing what Greta had deposited in the bottom of her golden cage, I realized the magic had deserted her as well.

"It comes to this," Dame Sniggett wailed.

"Didn't anybody miss me?" inquired the bald-headed man.

"I assume, good sir, that you are the uncle," Ebenezum said after a particularly hearty nose blow.

"And who might you be, sir?" the bald-headed man replied. "Sniggie, you haven't been going around hiring any extra servants?" He examined Ebenezum's silver-embroidered robes. "Unless you aren't— Sir, just what are you doing alone in this house with my wife!"

"Indeed," Ebenezum rumbled. He stooped to gather up my pack amidst the now scattered chicken cages, then thrust it in my arms. He turned, his wizardly strides taking him quickly from the room.

I risked a final glance at the lovely Ferona, but she was lost to me, crying over a mound of gray brown where once there had been a pile of gold.

"You'll pay for this!" Dame Sniggett shrieked at my master's retreating back. "This is not proper at all!"

"Enough of that lot," the mage muttered when we were free of the house. "May all their gold change in turn." He nodded at a man in the robes of a monk who walked toward us. "Rather we should use our magic to aid the pilgrims the girl was always going on about."

"I agree entirely." The monk smiled and pulled back his cowl. Even with the shaven head, I could tell it was Bork.

"Decided it was time for a change," he said to our inquiring glances. "A quieter life, free from the petty pursuits of the material world. Besides"—he tugged at his sleeve—"these fine, thick robes come with the job."

Brother Bork chose to walk with us a ways, and Ebenezum summarized the events that had transpired after his departure.

"You are holier than I," Bork said at last. "You banished every last bit of the curse, and used up the only remedy known to prevent your malady, then left the estate without any sort of payment whatever?"

"I didn't say that," Ebenezum replied. He poked the pack I carried with two fingers. Something clucked.

"A chicken?" Bork asked.

"Dinner." Ebenezum nodded. "Would you care to join us?"

I blanched. Somehow, the thought of a chicken dinner did not appeal to me at all. Quite understandable, I should think, considering what I had been through, even though the werespell over me had vanished with the rest of the gifts from the Netherhells. No, no chicken for me. I would content myself with the bag of dried corn I had brought with me from the estate. Amazingly enough, before this afternoon I had never realized how incredibly tasty dried corn could be.

But we were out in the open, on our way to Vushta again. Quite naturally, it was only a matter of moments before we were attacked by yet another band of assassins.

NINE

*"Wizards, like all mortals, need their rest.
Casting spells, righting wrongs, and putting a
little away for your old age can all be draining
occupations. The true wizard must therefore
always insist on a good night's sleep, and a few
days' respite between tasks. After some particularly grueling work, a couple of weeks in the
country are not out of line. In the aftermath of
truly major assignments, of course, nothing less
than a seaside vacation will do. And what of
those situations in which a wizard's work affects
the very world around him, perhaps the fabric of
the cosmos itself? Well, be advised that prime
accommodations in Vushta must be reserved at
least two months in advance."*

—THE TEACHINGS OF EBENEZUM,
Volume XXIII

It was all too much. I could barely support the pack
upon my back. Its weight had surely increased four-

fold. I leaned on my stout oak staff with such force that it bent each time I put my weight against it. I was sure it soon would snap. My feet barely lifted from the ground as I walked, and I stumbled over hidden rocks and roots as we made our slow way down what passed for a path. Sometime during our exhausted flight, we seemed to have wandered entirely away from the main highway and now found ourselves on a trail so overgrown that even the forest animals seemed to have given up on it.

As tired as I was, Ebenezum was more exhausted still. His head was bowed, his back was bent. His once wizardly strides had shortened to a very unwizardly hobble.

When we had first departed Dame Sniggett's after the successful resolution of her chicken problem, all had seemed well with my master. The tiredness that had ensued after his first use of the remedial herbs seemed to have passed him by entirely on the second application. The wizard began to talk expansively about the possibility of a cure, especially after we obtained another quantity of the healing poultice.

But my master spoke prematurely. His second reaction to the drug came after we had been on the road two full days and was fully four times worse than his earlier reaction. His first response, after our battle with Tork, had been exhaustion. His response after our chicken incident made exhaustion seem like a highly active state.

Then, of course, there were our constant encounters with assassins. And did I mention the increasing incidence of earthquakes? At first I thought it was my balance going, following my muscles into the blanket of fatigue. But no, we were plagued by ever-increasing tremors, as if giants were stomping foothills into the earth. These left us shaken at the least, and often not standing at all.

Ebenezum stumbled forward, managing at last to stand reasonably still. He paused and turned to me, his eyes once so capable of wizardly rage and sorcerous persuasion now no more than red and tired.

"Rest," was all he said.

I pointed to a likely group of stones on the far side of the path where we might sit for a while. We made our way over to them as best we could. I removed my pack with rather less grace than I would have liked. I decided not to look inside it just yet. I would discover what had broken at some later time.

Ebenezum didn't even notice the noise. He was too busy sitting down, which, like everything else just then, occupied a great amount of his time. He groaned and exhaled at the same instant, as if in the process of sitting he might release all his problems to the four winds.

We sat for a long moment in silence. My master's labored breathing softened over time. At last, he pushed back his cap to look at me.

"I was afraid of this," he said. "A second use of that potion has drained all the vitality from my body. 'Twould kill me to use it again." My master paused to regain his wind.

"What are we to do?" I asked before I realized that the wizard had again dozed where he sat.

I knew then it was up to me. Ebenezum was exhausted beyond all imagining. I must find someplace he could rest and recover.

"Pardon?" said a voice from across the road.

I looked up quickly. Two heavily cloaked figures stood a scant yard away.

"Did I say something?" I inquired.

"Oh, no." One of the cloaked figures stepped forward. Only his hands were visible, but they waved about wildly as he spoke, as if they wished to escape the cloak that hid the rest of him.

"I said 'pardon,' " he continued, "for I wish to speak with you. You must excuse me, for I have not the social graces of conversation. For you see, I am but a poor hermit, and seldom speak at all."

The speaker pulled back his hood, revealing a round, bald head that shone in the afternoon sun.

"Oh," I replied after I deciphered his conversation. "And you wished to say something to me?"

"Most assuredly, yes." His hands darted about to indicate his chest. "As I have stated, I am but a poor hermit and religious seeker, Heemat by name, pledged for twenty years never to utter a word. Yes, for twenty years these lips are sealed, never to groan in pain or laugh with joy. But that is of no consequence, for when I saw the two of you by the side of the road, I found 'twas time to break my vow."

Heemat continued to smile. I looked to my master, but the wizard snored lightly upon his rock. He had managed to sleep through all of this. It was only then that I realized how truly fatigued Ebenezum was.

Well, tired though I was in turn, someone would have to see this situation through. And I would do it in a way that would make my master proud. I stared at this bald, smiling fellow. Something about him struck me as peculiar. Now, I thought, how would Ebenezum handle this?

"Indeed," I said, determined to seek this hermit's true nature. "You are a religious seeker?"

"Yes," Heemat replied, lifting his hands to the skies. "I follow the lesser deity, Plaugg the Fairly Magnificent."

"Indeed." I decided I would leave this particular point for the nonce. "And are you sworn to silence for twenty years?"

"Well, yes, more or less. But as we walked down this road to see the two of you in such obvious need . . ."

The hermit's voice trailed away. Such obvious need? I coughed.

"We were just resting."

"Your companion looks like he might rest for the next dozen years."

I looked over at Ebenezum. He had managed, somehow, to curl up on top of his boulder. His snoring grew louder.

"Just a short afternoon nap," I replied, trying to keep the anxiety out of my voice. How was I to wake the wizard up, short of kicking him?

"Well, perhaps you need a place to stay until his nap is completed?" Heemat waved to his left. "Our hovel is just down the road a bit."

That's it. Now I knew what was bothering me. I stroked my chin thoughtfully. "Indeed," I remarked. "You say you are a hermit, sir."

"That's correct."

"Well." I coughed gently. "Since when do hermits have traveling companions?" I had to keep myself from smiling. What logic! My master would have been proud of me.

"I see." Heemat's hands retreated within his robes at the very hint of impropriety in his conduct. "I believe custom is somewhat different here than wherever you come from. I can tell you are a traveler."

I was completely undone. "In this country, hermits travel in pairs?"

"Come, come. There's no reason to belabor the

obvious. How come you to this place?''

"Well, we seem to have wandered off the main road somewhere back there," I admitted before I regained my composure. "A second! Why does your companion not speak? Has he taken a vow of silence as well?"

"Snarks, here?" Heemat laughed, the smile fully across his face again. "No, no, he's never taken a vow in his life. He just doesn't like to talk. Isn't that right, Snarks?"

The other figure nodded and said something from deep within his folds of cloak. It sounded like "Mmrrpphh!"

Somehow, all these explanations were doing nothing to reassure me. "What did your friend say?" I demanded.

"Sounded like 'mmrrpphh' to me." Heemat rubbed his belly happily.

There really was something all wrong here. I cursed my lack of experience. Maybe I should go over and shake Ebenezum awake.

With that, the wizard rolled off his boulder bed into a mass of brambles immediately behind the stone. His sleeping form sank from sight, but his snoring grew louder still.

"Our hovel *is* just down the road." Heemat shrugged. "Of course, he could sleep in the brambles all night, if that is your preference."

I looked from the hermit to his cloaked companion. Snarks waved his gloved hands above his head and shouted something like "Vrrmmpphh!"

Someone tapped me on the shoulder.

An attack from the rear! I spun about all too quickly, almost losing my balance in the process. So, after all this talk, they would finally make their move! These fiends were everywhere! If only I could discern the true nature of their hellish schemes. I knew magic now! I would fight them if I must, whether they numbered two or two hundred!

The newcomer was a good two feet taller than myself, dressed entirely in black. His shoulders were incredibly broad as well. You could have fit two normal men side by side and just matched the width of his frame. His face was pale and without amusement. He spoke in the deepest voice I had ever heard.

"I need some assistance."

With that, a new earthquake hit. If the earlier quakes had been a giant stamping his foot, this one was the annual giant's dancing social. We were, all but the tall man, tossed to the ground by the severity of it.

It was over in a second. I glanced at the boulders. Apparently, Ebenezum was still asleep.

A great, trumpeting cry came from the depth of the woods. The large man spun about with the grace one might expect of a dancer or a professional eel catcher.

A huge wild boar broke from the underbrush. The creature was larger than I was tall, with great, sharp tusks that seemed pointed straight in my direction. It bellowed again as it raced across the clearing, intent on its frenzied attack. My stout oak staff suddenly felt very puny in my hands.

The large man stepped in the wild boar's path. The boar kept coming straight for him. The man in black grabbed the two tusks as if the huge pig were offering them rather than attacking. He calmly flipped the creature over as he stepped aside. Before the boar could recover, the large man had placed his immense hand around the pig's equally huge neck and lifted the beast aloft. The boar roared, then made an odd, choking sound as the large man squeezed its windpipe. When the boar stopped struggling, the large man casually tossed it back into the woods.

"I do like strangling wild pigs," he remarked. "It's such a satisfying feeling." He flexed his muscles absently.

Then again, perhaps fighting with this fellow wasn't such a good idea. But I couldn't run away, either, and leave Ebenezum snoring in the shrubbery.

"Indeed," I said.

"Well, no matter," the large man said. "I seem to have wandered off the main road somehow, and it will interfere with my duties."

"Alas, another lost traveler!" Heemat exclaimed. "Perhaps we can be of service."

"Who's this?" the large man asked softly.

"Only Heemat, good sir." Heemat spread his hands before him. "A poor hermit and religious pilgrim, pledged to Plaugg the Moderately Glorious. I have only recently broken a vow of silence to aid—"

"That's enough." The large man lifted a very large hand by his large head.

Heemat's smiling mouth snapped shut.

"Who's this?" The large man nodded toward the hermit's cloaked companion.

"Wvvxxrrgghh." Snarks took a rapid step to the rear.

"That is Snarks, sir," I quickly interjected. "Heemat's traveling companion."

"Wait a second," the large man said. "How can you be a hermit and have a traveling companion?"

Heemat's well-clothed form grew rigid. "I will not

be swayed by the narrow-minded dictates of so-
ciety!" he cried.

"Very well." The large man shrugged his incredibly broad shoulders. Heemat smiled apologeti-
cally.

"I am known as"—the large man made a sound
like an elderly woman being bludgeoned to death by
an unwilling snake—"although very few people can
pronounce that. I am known, more simply, as the
Dealer of Death."

"Indeed," I replied, recalling the great speed with
which he had dispatched the rampaging pig. "And
what can we do for you, Great Dealer of Death?"

"My friends call me the Dealer," the Dealer replied. "I am on a sacred quest, to find and kill the
enemy of my employer, King Urfoo the Vengeful."
Casually, the Dealer cracked his massive knuckles.

King Urfoo? A chill went down my spine as a certain clarity began returning to my head. My tired feet
suddenly felt capable of running once again. King
Urfoo?

"Ah, a sacred quest." Heemat nodded his head
knowingly.

"Bzzgllphfll," Snarks added.

"Yes, I must find a certain wizard."

"A wizard?" I inquired. The chill seemed to have
spread across my entire rib cage. I was, at last, fully
and most completely awake.

"Ebenezum is his name," the Dealer remarked.

"Indeed?" My voice had suddenly become much
higher. I thought it best to cease speaking altogether.

The Dealer of Death turned to the hermit and his
companion. The muscles in the Dealer's neck rippled
as he spoke.

"You know of no one by that name?"

"Wsspklblgg," Snarks mused.

"No, sir, we are not personally acquainted with the gentleman," Heemat added as he backed away.

"Alas." The Dealer sighed. His rib cage danced as the muscles contracted. "My quest must continue."

A particularly loud snore came from amidst the brambles.

"What is that?" The Dealer looked about him, a grim smile playing about his lips. "Another wild pig that needs to be strangled?"

"No, sir!" I cried. " 'Twas nothing! Just a forest bird!"

Ebenezum moaned in his sleep, then snored again.

"You're sure it's not a pig?" the Dealer asked wistfully. "Sounds too deep for a bird. I do rather enjoy strangling pigs."

We paused for a moment but heard nothing but birds and the rustling of small forest animals. Ebenezum was mercifully silent.

"Oh, well, I must get back to the main road, then." The Dealer snatched a passing butterfly and ripped it in two. "Not as much fun as killing a pig," he muttered.

Heemat gave the large man directions on how to regain the highway. The Dealer waved to us all and started back the way he came, his stride three times that of a normal person. My breathing began to return to normal.

"Well, Snarks." Heemat waved to his companion. "Apparently no one wants our hospitality."

"A minute!" I cried, turning away from the rapidly retreating Dealer. "I have reconsidered. We shall make use of your hospitality after all."

"Ah, splendid!" Heemat clapped his hands to-

gether. "You realize, of course, that there is a small
fee involved."

I nodded absently. I had made my decision at last,
and I would not sway from it. Ebenezum was in no
condition to travel, and though I still could not quite
bring myself to trust the hermit, whatever his hovel
offered had to be better than facing the Dealer of
Death.

"I don't imagine we can wake your friend." Heemat nodded in the general direction of the brambles.
"No matter. We'll get him there. Of course, this en-
tails a slight portage fee."

I nodded again. With the Dealer of Death gone, I
found my weariness was quickly returning. The three
of us walked to the back of the stone.

"Come! We shall carry him!" Heemat and Snarks
proceeded to disengage the wizard from the surrounding brambles.

There was a firm tap at my shoulder.

"Excuse me," the Dealer of Death said, "but I
seem to have gotten myself turned about completely.
Oh! Here's someone I haven't seen before. Aren't
those wizard's robes?"

Ebenezum woke up and sneezed.

TEN

"The common folk have many sayings, all about it being darkest before the dawn and clouds with silver linings and suchlike. We in the magical trade like to express our opinions of these matters somewhat differently. A lifetime of experience will have taught the average sorcerer that no matter how hopeless the situation seems, no matter how painful and fraught with danger his options may be, no matter how close he may be to an indescribably hideous death and perhaps even eternal damnation, still, the good wizard knows, it can always get far worse."

—THE TEACHINGS OF EBENEZUM,
Volume XLVI (General Introduction)

"Msstplckt!" Snarks cried.

"Gesundheit," the Dealer added as the hermit's companion ran away.

"Thank you." Ebenezum blew his nose on his sleeve. "And whom do I have the honor of addressing?"

"This is the Dealer of Death, master," I hastily interjected, "sent on a mission by one King Urfoo."

"Indeed?" Ebenezum struggled up to a sitting position, pulling a dozen briers along with him. "Help me up, would you, Wuntvor?"

I did as I was asked.

"So you're the Dealer of Death?" the wizard reiterated.

The Dealer made the woman-being-pummeled-at-some-length noise again. And Ebenezum repeated it.

The Dealer said he was impressed by my master's facility. Ebenezum remarked that he had some small learning. Wasn't the Dealer an acolyte of the respected "noise-rather-like-a-group-of-chickens-being-attacked-by-a-dozen-rakes" sect?

The Dealer was overjoyed that Ebenezum had heard of his order and began to talk rapidly about his teachers, all of whom had names that sounded as if someone were being strangled and torn to shreds simultaneously. The relief I had felt at my master's sudden recovery was once again turning to anxiety. I had very pointedly dropped Urfoo's name into the conversation when I had introduced them. Still, it was quite possible that the wizard did not know the great degree of danger he was in. How could I warn Ebenezum without giving his identity away to the large killer he now spoke to?

"But enough of this cheerful gossip!" the Dealer cried. "I do not even know your name. What knowledgeable man am I now addressing?"

"My good sir," Ebenezum said. I tugged violently

at his sleeve. "Not now, Wuntvor, I'm talking. As I was saying, I am—"

The earth shook once again. The giants' social dance had become a once-a-year gala festival. Even the Dealer fell this time.

There was a roaring in the woods. Eagerly, the Dealer of Death regained his footing.

A very large brown bear crashed through the undergrowth. The Dealer smiled. He raised a hand as if he would wave at the eight-foot-high, fear-crazed beast. The bear, sensing an easy target, rushed him.

His hand came down sharply on the bear's skull as the beast approached. There was a sharp crack. The Dealer stepped back to avoid the bear's still-swinging claws. The bear, now deceased, fell to the floor of the clearing.

"That's quite impressive," Ebenezum remarked.

"It was nothing," replied the Dealer, wiping bear's brains from his hand with a fallen leaf. "But when we were so rudely interrupted, you were introducing yourself?"

"Ah, yes." Ebenezum smiled as he straightened his robes. The end was near. I held my breath as I waited to hear the wizard's last words before his very speedy assassination. I wondered absently if his brains would be a different color from those of the bear.

"As I was saying," the wizard continued, "I am unable to divulge that information at this time. Like you, sir, I am on a mission."

The Dealer nodded his head. "I knew you were a kindred spirit all along."

"We are all kindred spirits!" Heemat cried, waving his hands to include the whole group of us and perhaps the entire forest beyond. "That is why Snarks and I stumbled upon you, and began this whole remarkable chain of events."

This was just too much. With the recent dramatic occurrences, I had almost forgotten the hermit and his cloaked companion. I began to say so when the wizard waved me to silence.

"We are quite assured of your importance," Ebenezum remarked. "Isn't it time you led us to your hovel?"

Heemat clapped his hands. "Of course! It's a very nice hovel, you'll see. Quite worth the pittance I ask for your stay."

I was astonished that my master would trust these two strangers so completely.

"Wunt, gather up the packs," my master instructed before I could say another word. In a lower voice, he remarked: "They are even more important than they think. And I do need my sleep."

I glanced up at the Dealer as I reassembled our gear. He, in turn, had furrowed his muscular brow as he gazed at the late afternoon sky.

"I think I shall come along as well," he remarked. "I do not care to be out alone after dark."

"Good! Good! A full hovel is a happy hovel!" Heemat cried as he turned to lead the way.

Ebenezum waved Snarks away as the hooded figure approached. "Keep your distance, would you? That's a good fellow. I need some space for proper contemplation." He wiped his nose on his sleeve, then paused for me to come abreast. "It has been an interesting trip so far," he whispered to me, "but I fear it will become far more interesting still, before the day is out."

I nodded and continued to walk down the path after Heemat. I found myself not so much interested as thoroughly confused. I was glad that Ebenezum was once again alert and in control.

With that thought, I felt the earth shift beneath me again.

"Wsstppllkt!" Snarks cried as a fissure opened at my feet. I found my stout oak staff torn from my trembling hands as the small cloaked figure ran down the length of the crack in the earth, swiping at things that tried to rise from the dust-filled fissure. The things cried out as they were struck, inhuman squeals of outrage, guttural cries of anger and pain.

The earth shook again and the fissure closed. Snarks walked back over and handed me my staff.

"Vllmmpp!" he remarked.

"Anytime," I replied, still somewhat shaken.

'Most interesting," Ebenezum mused behind me. "Just what I thought."

With that, the procession resumed its march in the fading evening light, winding its way along the barely existing path to Heemat's.

"All hail Plaugg, the Reasonably Grandiose!" Heemat intoned. "Welcome to my humble hovel." He waved as two women dressed in forest garb passed us in the front hallway, then stopped abruptly as we reached a table, behind which stood a third man wearing a hermit's cloak. Heemat studied the wall beyond the third hermit, then turned back to us.

"I'm afraid the only cells that I have to offer you are way over in the south wing. 'Tis the busy season in the forest, after all. They're quite nice accommodations, mind you, just don't get as much sun as those cells in the east and north. I'll block your rooms all in a group, so you may continue your discussions!''

He turned back to the third hermit. ''Maurice, see what you can do for our guests, won't you?'' He waved to all of us as he walked away. ''Maurice will show you your rooms.'' He coughed delicately as he passed through one of the surrounding doorways. ''He will, of course, also make arrangements for payment.''

With that, he was gone. I noticed that Snarks had disappeared somewhere as well, so that only Ebenezum, the Dealer, and myself stood before Maurice, a thin man with a mustache, who proceeded to read us rates from a large red ledger. The Dealer claimed to be without funds, as was the practice of his sect. Perhaps, I hoped wildly, we could be free of him at last. Ebenezum reached into one of the many folds in his wizardly robes and paid for all three of us.

I did my best not to show my dismay. The black-clad man followed us down the hall, idly squashing insects that here and there crawled along the walls. Was my master trying to kill us all?

''I am indebted to you,'' the large man rumbled as Maurice opened the door to our suite of cells. The mustached hermit hovered behind us as we inspected our new quarters, as if he expected something more from us. A single, dark look from the Dealer sent Maurice on his way.

''Again,'' the Dealer addressed Ebenezum, ''thank you for your generosity. Most times my sect has little need for money. Gold, like all worldly things, would interfere with our art.''

By way of emphasis for the last remark, the Dealer leapt in the air, twisted about in a somersault, and landed facing us on the room's far side.

"Very impressive." The wizard stroked his beard. "Still, it might be better if you ceased your demonstrations until you were once again outside. I believe you have landed on the room's only table."

The Dealer looked down at the splinters that clustered about his feet. "Once again, I am in your debt. Most times, my sect has little need for furniture. Tables, like all wordly things, would interfere with our art."

"Indeed," Ebenezum replied. "But you pursue your art now, do you not, on a sacred mission?"

The Dealer kicked what remained of the table out of the way. "You are a man of understanding, sir. For I have signed a contract with King Urfoo to kill a wizard and his two traveling companions." A grim smile lit the fellow's broad and muscular face. "And when my sect signs a contract, the dividend is death." He began to move his arm as if he might punch through the wall, then stopped himself.

"Excuse me," he remarked. "I become overly enthusiastic when discussing my art."

"Perfectly understandable," Ebenezum said as he sat in a rough-hewn chair, the room's only remaining piece of furniture. "But I am curious. How does one sign a death pact?"

The Dealer smiled gleefully. "One negotiates. You must be very clever. It is the final lesson of my sect."

"Indeed. It must be difficult to negotiate with royalty."

The Dealer nodded, still smiling.

"Especially with someone like Urfoo. I hear he is

very tight with the purse strings."

"He is a clever bargainer, no doubt about it. But we Dealers of Death are cleverer still. After I kill the wizard and his two assistants, one very young, the other very fat, I need only return to Urfoo and pay him ten pieces of gold!"

Both Ebenezum and I stared at the large man for a moment. So this was how Urfoo, stingiest of monarchs, finally hired a qualified assassin!

"I was very clever," the Dealer continued. "Originally, Urfoo only had me pay a single gold piece for each of the three I kill. But the job is worth far more than that!"

"Indeed," Ebenezum said softly. "You are paying Urfoo so he can have you kill three persons?"

"Why, yes, those are the terms of the contract." The Dealer's well-muscled mouth turned downward. "Isn't that the proper method? Do you mean . . ."

He frowned deeply, then stamped his foot in frustration. The room shook. "Wouldn't you just know it! It was almost graduation. Who would blame anyone for skimping a little on the final course of study? I did learn all the definitions, just had a little trouble with addition and subtraction. I pay him, he pays me, what does it matter? A contract is a contract. Negotiations interfere with my art!"

The Dealer punched his fist into the ceiling. His knuckles left indentations in the rock. "I find this place confining. I will return in time for dinner."

With that, the large man was gone.

When I was sure the Dealer was well away from the room, I asked my master just what he was doing.

"There are many kinds of problems, Wuntvor," Ebenezum intoned. "There are small ones that occur every day, and are easily dealt with. Then, there are the larger problems, that one must plan in order to conquer. Finally, there are a few problems so enormous that the only way to deal with them is to ignore them completely and go about your other business. Our friend the Dealer falls into this latter category."

How could my master be so calm? "But shouldn't we run away?"

"The minute we run, he will realize who we are. We are far safer as his friends. You see, I know even more about his sect than I discussed with the Dealer. They are commonly known as the Urracht."

"The Urracht?"

Ebenezum nodded. "The sound the victim makes after they see the assassin. The last sound they make."

"Urracht," I repeated. The word felt cold in my throat.

"Very efficient assassins, trained for years in the arts of death. Every effort is turned toward murder, so much effort, in fact, that there is little room in their lives for anything else."

I pondered my master's words.

"Do you mean they are somewhat deficient in wit?"

"Much as a large fern is deficient. Or perhaps a multifaceted piece of quartz. Every time they look for their feet, their shoes get in the way. In other words, yes. And as long as we act as a nonsuspicious pair, rather than the fugitive trio the Dealer is looking for, I imagine we will be quite safe."

The room shook again.

"Then again," Ebenezum remarked, "life is not so predictable as our assassin."

I braced myself, waiting for the quake to come. But the room shook in a way different from the tremors we had felt for the past few days. The shocks came with a regular rhythm, as if someone were trying to pound through the walls. And there was a voice, crying something far away, a single word over and over again.

It took me a long moment to recognize that word, but once I did, I knew the voice as well.

Deep and sepulchral, it rang in my ears:

"Doom! Doom! Doom!"

ELEVEN

"Nothing is quite so unexpected as the truth. If, for example, you find your spells inadequate to defeat the local dragon, immediately go to your employers and apologize profusely. They should be so taken aback by your show of humility that you will have plenty of time to hastily vacate the area, allowing the dragon to eat your employers rather than you, and thus halt any ugly rumors they might have spread about your competence."

—THE TEACHINGS OF EBENEZUM,
Volume XXXIII

The wizard and I looked at each other for a long moment, the only sound the warrior's distant, muffled cries. So Hendrek was lodging here as well! But what if Hendrek ran into the Dealer of Death? From our former dealings with Hendrek, we knew he was not a subtle man. And should the Dealer of Death see the three of us together . . . well, even the large Urracht assassin couldn't be that stupid, could he?

"Doom!"

Ebenezum sighed, his eyes still half-shut with fatigue.

"Wuntvor," he whispered. "See what can be done."

I left the room as Ebenezum sat heavily on the bed. It was up to me, then, to find the large warrior and silence his cries.

"Doom!"

The word echoed down the corridor. I turned left, headed toward the sound.

"Doom!" I prayed the Dealer had by now found the forest and a brace of pigs to be strangled. Truly, Hendrek could not make his presence more well known if he had painted arrows along the corridor. He cried out again, and the sound reverberated against the walls. What would make the big man shout that way?

Demons, of course.

I slowed my headlong rush to meet the warrior. I had run into the midst of sorcerous dealings before. I did not wish to repeat my error. Perhaps stealth was called for here rather than haste.

A small, sickly-colored creature, dressed in a checkered suit, stepped in my path. It waved a cigar in my direction. It was Smilin' Brax.

"Ah, we meet again," the demon intoned from behind the broadest smile I had ever seen. "Never forget a potential customer. Rule number one of demonic commerce. And believe me, young sir, never have you needed the services of a charmed weapons dealer as you do now."

The conviction in the demon's voice chilled me. I temporarily forgot my quest to stare at the cheerful creature. What terrible secret could make Brax that happy?

"And you notice that I call my weapons charmed." Brax took a puff on its cigar. "Because my previously owned weapons are truly charming. And you, good sir, are in luck! I'm overstocked! I've just received a huge inventory from a tribe of nature worshipers. I don't know what came over me! I don't have room for them in my warehouse. I'm almost giving weapons away!"

Hendrek's voice echoed again from somewhere in the hermit's massive hovel. Brax's smile faltered for only an instant. The demon waved the cigar in my direction.

"You look like a young man of unusual intelligence," the creature remarked. "And I'm about to make you an unusual offer. You won't be sorry you listened to me. I see you carry a walking staff. Small stuff, I assure you. Have you ever thought really big? Why walk around with a puny branch, when you can own an entire magic tree?"

"Magic tr—" I began.

"I see the idea appeals to you! Yes, just think of it, a magic tree, straight from the nature worshipers of the North. And just barely broken in, I can assure you, only used for an occasional human sacrifice, and those only on the solstices! Someday, young man, you will be a sorcerer. Just think of the amazing tactical advantages if you came to your sorcerous battles accompanied by a tree!"

"Doom!" The cry was far closer now.

"Yes, yes, of course, we also carry more conventional weapons," Brax added hurriedly as he edged toward the middle of the hall. "Perhaps there is some question in your mind about obtaining something as large as a tree for your first mystical weapon. Although, may I assure you, the surprise value alone of such a weapon—"

Headbasher came flying down the hall.

"Urk!" the demon cried as it dodged the club. Hendrek followed his weapon at a run.

"Doom!" he cried as he spied us both.

"Friend Hendrek!" the demon replied in a somewhat less friendly voice than before. "I must protest your business practices! I have told you before, I will not accept a return of your enchanted weapon, no matter how forcefully"—the demon dodged Headbasher, now in Hendrek's hands—"you attempt to thrust it upon me. A contract is a contract."

Hendrek's club crashed into the wall quite close to the demon's head. I ducked as stone shards flew over me. I heard other voices in the distance, then the sound of running feet. Our little altercation seemed to be attracting some attention.

"Really, good Hendrek." Brax spoke rapidly, dodging the warrior's blows with even more dexterity than the last time I had seen them meet. "I am not unsympathetic to your plight. So you did not read the fine print on your contract." The demon dashed between the warrior's legs, temporarily freezing the large man. "A purely human error, nothing you should blame yourself for. But I, after all, am in the business of human error. And I urge you to pay your contract."

Hendrek regained his bearings and spun on the small fiend in checkerboard garb.

"I have done all I can, yelp!" the demon cried as the weapon grazed his shoulder. "All I ask is that you depose a minor ruler or assassinate a fairly ineffectual high priest. That would be payment enough for now. If you continue to refuse, I'm afraid the matter will be out of my hands. I'll be forced to send the Dread Collectors!"

Hendrek paused in his attack.

"The Dread Collectors?"

The demon nodded silently. "My hands are tied. There is nothing else I can do."

"I didn't know about the Dread Collectors," Hendrek whispered. "Doom."

The running footsteps grew closer. I glanced around to see Heemat and Snarks speeding toward us, their robes flapping with their haste.

"Yzzzgghhtt!" Snarks cried.

"You!" Brax replied, his smile replaced by a look of pure loathing.

"Doom!" Hendrek replied, once again raising his club above his head.

"Excuse me," an even more sepulchral voice intoned by my side. I jumped involuntarily. Suddenly, the Dealer of Death had appeared silently in our midst. "Somehow, in trying to find the exit, I lost my way in this vast maze of hallways." He glanced at Hendrek. "Ah! A fellow warrior!"

Club still over head, Hendrek regarded the newcomer with some suspicion.

"And what have we here!" Heemat jumped into our midst. "A large number of guests at my humble hovel, all engaged in social discourse!" He smiled at us all, his hands rubbing together fast enough to generate heat. "But I venture that few of you have yet experienced a number of the humble pleasures available at our little retreat. Have any of us visited the lower level yet today? No? Well, let me recommend our fabulous casino tavern, with entertainment nightly by the Hovellettes. And what of our temperature-controlled swimming pond—"

"Fellow warrior?" the Dealer of Death mused. "You wouldn't happen to know someone named Hendrek, would you? About your size, from what I understand."

With an unearthly shriek, Brax jumped upon the heavily cloaked Snarks.

"And have I mentioned our sun roof?" Heemat continued.

"Trrf blggllzz!"

"You have cost me too many sales, demon!" Brax screamed. "They were too kind to merely banish you from the Netherhells! Now I shall banish you from this world as well!"

"Excuse me," the Dealer of Death murmured to Hendrek. "We should continue our conversation in a moment. It occurs to me that I haven't strangled a demon in some months."

Before I could see him move, his hand was around Brax's throat.

"Urracht!" Brax cried. "That's a very powerful grip you have there, sir."

The Dealer smiled. "Prepare to meet your death, demon."

"Have you considered how much more powerful you'd be with an enchanted weapon in that hand?"

The Dealer tightened his grip.

"Urk! Just asking! Easy credit terms!"

With a soft pop, the demon disappeared.

The Dealer grunted as his hand closed into a fist.

"That's the trouble with demons," he muttered. "You just get a good strangle started, and they disappear. No manners at all."

"There, there!" Heemat beamed. "Nasty things, demons, but it's gone now. Why don't we retire to the Hovel Lounge, where we can play a quick game of Hovelo?"

The Dealer flexed his fingers. "An awful feeling, losing something midstrangle. Makes you want to grab the nearest free creature and throttle him just so the effort isn't wasted."

"Hovelo is a fascinating game," Heemat continued. "And so easy to play! A bean is placed in one of three identical cups . . ."

He paused as the Dealer placed a hand on his shoulder.

"It takes a great effort of will not to strangle something," the Dealer whispered. "I would appreciate some quiet."

"Certainly!" Heemat's hands flew back within his robes. "Snarks, we should go and prepare this evening's entertainment."

A voice even more muffled than before mumbled something from the corner of the hallway. The small hermit seemed to have become completely entangled in his robes during his battle with Brax. Head and feet were absolutely indistinguishable within the mass of torn fabric. Some part of him bumped repeatedly against the wall.

"Llffmm," Snarks cried weakly.

"Doom," Hendrek replied. "The little fellow may be suffocating! Quick. Help me free him from his robes."

"No, no!" Heemat cried. "You don't understand, his sacred vows . . ."

But his protests were too late, for the immense warrior and the Dealer of Death had rushed to either side of the fallen hermit and were pulling the small man's clothes away in opposite directions.

There was a long, loud rip. Snarks's head popped

out of what had once been his clothing. His head was green and had a pair of horns, one above each ear.

"A demon!" the Dealer cried.

"Doom!" replied Hendrek.

"This is not what you think—" Snarks the demon began. Hendrek's club smashed into the pile of formerly occupied robes. The now naked Snarks was halfway down the hall.

The demon cleared this throat politely. "You'd do better, you know, if you anticipated your opponent's movements before blindly striking."

"Doom!" Hendrek cried even more loudly. He twirled the enchanted Headbasher above his head until the warclub sang.

"And you know," Snarks continued as he ran, "you could stand to lose a little weight."

"Doom!" Hendrek bellowed so loudly that I had to cover my ears. His immense bulk rushed the retreating demon.

"And do you mind if I ask you when the last time was that you managed to take a bath?"

Hendrek's rage went beyond words. The demon disappeared around a bend in the corridor, the warrior in heavy pursuit.

"Our shame is known!" Heemat cried, wringing his robes with both hands. "Snarks is a demon, but he is a different demon. He could not help it! When he was a small demon-child, his mother was frightened to death by the promises of a group of politicians. You can imagine the damage done to his impressionable young mind. He became everything those demon politicians were not. Yes, friends, now Snarks is ruled by a great compulsion to tell nothing but the truth! The absolute truth, in great detail, and

at great length, exploring every nuance that might occur to him, but the truth!''

'' 'Tis no wonder you keep him heavily cloaked.''

I looked up to see Ebenezum standing at the same
bend in the corridor where Snarks and Hendrek had
disappeared. The wizard blew his nose.

''Yes,'' Heemat admitted sadly. ''Praise Plaugg
the Moderately Exhalted, sometimes Snarks was too
much for even a humble hermit such as myself. Why,
do you know that one time he said I should stop moving my hands . . . and those things he inferred about
my smile, and my haircut!'' The hermit coughed
softly. ''Suffice it to say, heavy robes were preferable
to a strangled throat.''

''That,'' replied the Dealer of Death, ''is a matter
of opinion.''

Ebenezum yawned. ''Now that the excitement is
over, I think I shall return to my nap.'' He glanced at
Heemat, his great bushy eyebrows knitted in concern. ''It is something of a trial to sleep in this place.
I expect this to be reflected in our bill.''

The hermit waved his shaved head in dismay. ''I
assure you, this is most unusual! My hovel is usually
the most quiet place imaginable, a combination of
the best the forest has to offer with a few innovative
ideas Snarks brought with him from the Netherhells!
Together, they make a truly unique experience. Just
wait for tonight and the entertainment!''

''I would like some entertainment now,'' the
Dealer whispered. ''Could you show me the way to
the forest?''

''Most assuredly! Follow me.'' The hermit bustled
down the corridor.

''I will feel better when I have strangled something," the Dealer remarked as he silently followed the huffing Heemat.

Ebenezum turned to me when they were gone. "Quickly, Wunt, you must seek out Hendrek and calm him before he squashes Snarks. A demon who tells only the truth could be very useful in the time to come."

"Time to come?" I asked. "Do you mean Vushta?"

The wizard shook his head. "No. If we are ever to travel to Vushta, first we must survive this night." He tugged at his beard. "Wuntvor, I must get my sleep. While my affliction prevents my practice of sorcery, my wizardly intuition is still intact. That intuition, as much as anything, has kept us alive during our travels. And that intuition tells me that we must prepare today, for tonight none of us here will have time to sleep at all. Now go find Hendrek!"

I ran down the corridor, listening for the warrior's low cries and the boom of Headbasher hitting rock, rather than demons.

TWELVE

"It is a mistake to think of all demons as being exactly alike. Some are short while others are tall; some are yellow, others are blue; some are nasty and others are extremely nasty. Some of the nastiest are quite fast as well. Should you encounter one of these, it is a mistake to think at all. Much more appropriate are such responses as running, screaming, and the very rapid formulation of a last will and testament."

—THE TEACHINGS OF EBENEZUM, Volume IX

The noise was deafening. Three quick, thundering crashes, followed by a wild scream.

"Doo—doo—doo!"

I heard another voice talking quietly in the midst of all the chaos. As I ran toward the melee, I could make out phrases between the thuds and shouts.

"Really, if you just held that club . . ." ". . . time you rested, you're getting rather . . ." ". . . a really

179

good diet plan, even if it does come from the Netherhells . . ."

The crashing and screaming stopped. Again, I ceased my headlong run and peaked cautiously around the corner.

Hendrek sat in the hallway, his massive form propped against the far wall. His eyes stared through me, far beyond the limits of the hall.

"D-d-d-d-da," he whispered.

Snarks frowned and shook his head at the inert warrior.

"Your friend has become distraught," the demon remarked solemnly. "If he could have sat still and just heard me out, he might have realized I meant him no harm. But with these big fellows, it's always attack, attack, attack! Soon they simply work themselves over the edge. Pity."

Hendrek's great bulk quivered like pudding. He collapsed upon the floor with a thunderous crash. I ran to his side. Mercifully, he appeared to have lost consciousness.

The large warrior began to snore.

"Persistent fellow, isn't he?" Snarks brushed off his green-scaled arms. "Oh, if only he could see himself as others see him."

I approached the small demon warily, my stout oak staff held close to my chest. "What do you want?" I asked.

The demon sighed. "What does anyone want? Someone to love, the respect of one's peers, perhaps to achieve something special in one's brief span. The first two, I fear, are now beyond my grasp. My extreme honor has caused me to be banished from among my fellows. You know, you don't have to hold that staff of yours so tightly. I am no threat whatsoever. You weren't so cautious of me when my face was hidden by hermit's robes, were you?"

The demon was right. I relaxed my grip on the wood.

"And you know," the demon continued, "you could manage to stand up a little straighter. It would do wonders for your overall appearance."

I felt my fingers tighten again on my staff.

"Ah, there I go again, don't I?" Snarks shook its head sadly. "It really is quite out of my control, you know. Not only am I a demon, I'm a cursed demon. It all seems rather redundant, doesn't it?"

The demon turned, shaking its head sadly, and walked away down the hall. I took a step to follow, but the floor was no longer where I expected it to be.

When the tremor subsided, I picked myself up from where I had fallen. This new quake had been sharp and fast, and seemed to have left less damage than the last couple I had experienced. Still, it took me a moment to fully regain my balance.

Snarks waited patiently for me at the next bend in the hallway. The demon yawned.

"Of course," it said, "I knew this would come as well."

Before I could ask the demon just what it meant by that remark, it launched into a long and vivid description of my complexion and the various problems it perceived therein. Without thinking, my hands went to my face. I couldn't look that bad, could I? I had a large red blotch where? There were certain remedies, the demon continued, poultices concocted in the Netherhells for conditions even as severe as mine. Why, Snarks had used one of the formulas very successfully. In just a few days it had completely shrunk the pus-filled hillocks that had marred his countenance, and it had had the unexpected additional benefit of turning his skin an attractive shade of green.

We had reached the door to Snarks's cell at last. I wondered absently if there might be a large sack about somewhere that I might place over my head.

But I collected my thoughts as the demon clothed itself. There was far more at stake here than a few unsightly blemishes. I would take this far-too-honest creature to my master. Ebenezum would know what to do.

I told Snarks we must go see the wizard.

"Good!" it replied. "It is best if you are completely honest with me as well. An eye for an eye, as the old saying goes. But take it from one who knows: it is just amazing how the truth facilitates communication." The demon adjusted its robes as it spoke. "Just a moment here, and I shall be rrddrrff gglmmphggl."

The hood once again totally covered the demon's face.

I grabbed a portion of the hooded demon that I took for an arm and pulled him from the room. The sooner we saw Ebenezum, the sooner I could forget my problem skin.

"Doooooooom." A low moan came from the corridor where we had left Hendrek. Placing myself between him and Snarks, I approached the fallen warrior, who had managed to regain a sitting position.

"Doooom!" Hendrek fumbled for his enchanted warclub, but Headbasher was still beyond his enfeebled grasp. "A demon hermit! They are all around me! They haunt me wherever I go!"

"Kkssbrffmm!" Snarks replied.

Hendrek growled in response. I realized Heemat was right. By now, without Snarks's muffling robes, the immense warrior would once again be in a rage.

"No, Hendrek," I replied. "This demon is different. It was banished from the Netherhells. Now, like it or not, it is one of us."

"Trrff," added Snarks.

"Doom," Hendrek said shortly. He retrieved his club at last and used it to help him stand. Even that exertion seemed almost too much for him. He swayed perilously for a moment on regaining his feet, but somehow his large boots remained on the floor. He made no move to attack but glowered in the demon's direction.

"Doom," he added again.

"I'm taking our friend here to the wizard. He'll know what to do about this." I grabbed Snarks and once again led the way. Hendrek nodded glumly and followed.

Snarks removed his hood for a moment. "I expected all this, you know." One brief glance at Hendrek, and the hood was hastily back in place.

Feet ran rapidly down a side corridor. I turned to see Heemat approach.

"Praise Plaugg the Somewhat Omnipotent! The three of you together, walking as friends!"

"Doom!" Hendrek whispered to me. "These corridors seem a maze, and yet we encounter a new person every fifty paces. 'Tis an enchanted place. I would not be surprised if I were to turn a corner and run into myself!"

Hendrek was right. I had felt a growing sense of uneasiness, too. For an establishment of this size, we seemed to be having random encounters impossible within the laws of chance. But then, Heemat had mentioned that some of this place had been built according to plans from the Netherhells.

"But we must plan tonight's entertainment," Heemat continued. "If our gracious guests could excuse Snarks now, he could give me some much needed assistance in the preparations."

I was about to object when I smelled the sulfur.

"Doom!" Hendrek cried again, his warclub poised unsteadily over his head.

Brax stood in the hallway before us. The demon flicked a bit of cigar ash on the floor.

"Last chance, Hendrek."

"Doom." The warrior did not move.

"Very well," Brax replied. "You shall meet the Dread Collectors."

With that, the chessboard-costumed demon disappeared, and in its place stood something extremely large and incredibly ugly. It appeared to have at least nine heads of different shapes and sizes. All the heads, however, had very sharp looking teeth. Perhaps, it occurred to me, this thing was actually a "they."

It, or they, scraped half a dozen feet equipped with razor claws along the floor, gouging rivulets in the hard-packed earth. The heads spoke as one.

"We have come to collect you," they said. "Will you come quietly, or do we have to rend and tear?"

All nine heads smiled as they finished the sentence. I had the sudden feeling that rending and tearing were two of their favorite forms of recreation.

"Doom!" Hendrek replied. "Before you rend and tear, you will feel the wrath of Headbasher!"

The nine heads laughed as one. I did not find the sound cheerful in the least.

"Shall we?" one head, vaguely in the center of the monstrous mass, asked.

"After you," the remaining heads replied. As one, nine demonic mouths opened and howled.

That howl was like nothing I had ever heard, the death cries of a hundred birds, or a thousand rodents screaming as they are crushed underfoot. The sound hit us like a wave from one of the Great Seas, pushing me back down the hall. I felt as if the wailing force would tear the flesh from my body and only leave the bones behind. I realized, in that instant, that the Collectors might have come for Hendrek, but they would take the rest of us as well.

The sound filled my head. All I could think of was the wailing. The things were coming for us, a blur of motion, all claws and teeth and long, sharp, razor things; tails, perhaps, or maybe something else that had no name.

I managed to lift my staff. Perhaps I could beat back a head or two before they overwhelmed me. I was aware of the others around me. Although the fiends rushed toward us, I felt that time had slowed, allowing me to regard each of my fellows in turn and ponder some on my life as well.

Hendrek, grim and silent, held his club at the ready. Snarks had pulled back its hood and was staring at the approaching demon-thing with a look of contempt. The evil eye, I thought. Maybe our honest demon would give the Dread Collectors indigestion. I did not see Heemat until Hendrek moved, revealing the hermit's hiding place.

The howling rose in pitch. It would push my eyeballs straight back into their sockets. The things were almost on us now, their slavering jaws as wide as my staff was long. I prepared to strike.

Words carried over the howling, words punctuated by sneezing.

The shrieks of demon rage became shrieks of fear. The heads turned on each other, snapping and biting, scratching and clawing. A dark, foul-smelling liquid sprayed through the air. It was demon blood.

There was an explosion like thunder, just overhead. The Dread Collectors vanished.

"Doom," Hendrek murmured.

The wizard sat at the far end of the corridor, his eyes closed, his breathing rapid. Ebenezum was still far from being at his best. But his magic had saved us again.

It occurred to me then that I might have been able to use sorcery against the Dread Collectors as well. I stared blankly at my stout oak staff. I was so used to confronting demons with brute force that my use of magic in a situation such as this never entered my head. True, I still only knew a few spells, and I imagined a rain of dead fish would have done little to slow the Collectors' attack. Still, there might have been some other bit of magic I might have used, far more effective than the piece of wood I held in my hands. I would have to start thinking like a wizard.

Ebenezum groaned and slid farther onto the floor.

"Hendrek!" I called to the large warrior, who still stared blankly at the spot where the Dread Collectors had disappeared. "Help me get my master to his room. I fear Ebenezum still needs his rest."

"Excuse me," a voice said by my side.

I spun before I could think, my body still full of the fear brought by our recent demonic encounter. My staff held the full force of my weight behind it as it rammed into the Dealer's shoulder.

The staff shattered as if it were made of glass. Splinters littered the floor. The Dealer of Death seemed not to notice.

"Excuse me," he repeated. "I believe the time for proper introductions is in order. If our companions here"—he smiled graciously at the large warrior and the fallen wizard—"are Hendrek and Ebenezum, you, I imagine, must be named Wuntvor?"

I did not reply. My tongue felt like ice within my mouth.

"Come come, now," the Dealer chided. "If we have to conduct business here, the least we can do is remain on friendly terms. You'll find me a very reasonable man. I'll give you a much more colorful death than you ever imagined. You'd be amazed at the large number of options available."

Somehow, I didn't find the Dealer's reassurances at all comforting.

"There are, of course, the popular standards: strangulation, beheading, impalement, suffocation . . . You know, the classic deaths. But my cult features a large number of novelty murders as well. Take 'The Troll and the Shepherdess,' for instance. That's a very popular number, let me tell you."

Hendrek could take no more. His face, normally flushed, was now crimson with anger, in stark contrast to the paleness of his knuckles where they gripped the doomed warclub, Headbasher.

He rushed the Dealer in silence. Headbasher sought the assassin's skull, but the Dealer deflected the club with a skillful fist. There was a crash when club met fist, like stone against stone.

The Dealer winced and smiled as he blew on his hand. "Ah. A worthy opponent. I shall have my entertainment at last."

"Doom," was Hendrek's sole reply as his club once again flew through the air. The Dealer deflected the new blow with an open palm, the sound of a small boulder falling on paving stone. The Dealer of Death lashed out with a foot aimed at Hendrek's great armored stomach. The foot met Headbasher instead, which Hendrek had somehow twisted to protect his vitals. I heard the sound of a tree crashing in the forest.

The Dealer tried to distract the warrior with his fists, but wherever the assassin mounted an attack, Headbasher was there first. The club seemed almost a part of the large warrior's arms, an extra joint that Hendrek could flex, giving him twice the power and speed of a normal man.

Or mayhap, I thought, the club controlled the man. In my previous experience with the vast warrior, Hendrek had always had a tendency to lumber. Now, though, his great club flashing in his hands, parrying constant blows from the Dealer of Death, the huge man seemed to dance, pirouetting from one impossible defense to another unlikely attack, then back to defense again. With the club in his hands, the warrior himself appeared enchanted. The Dealer of Death was an extremely well trained assassin; but when he faced Hendrek, he faced magic.

The Dealer of Death seemed to be enjoying himself immensely, however. He would laugh with every blow of Headbasher, and his face was lit by a smile as innocent as a child's.

"Urracht against enchantment!" he cried at last. " 'Tis a fair game, 'twould seem, but I fear it's time to change the rules!"

He laughed, jumped to one side, landed on his

hands, then sprang to his feet behind the large warrior. Hendrek spun to defend himself again, but the
Dealer now stood over the unconscious Ebenezum.

"If I cannot kill the enchanted warrior," the
Dealer remarked, "I shall kill the enchanter instead.
You have to be flexible in my profession."

Hendrek raised his club threateningly.

"I do believe I can fend you off and kill someone
else at the same time," the Dealer continued. "In
fact, I consider it a bit of a challenge." He smiled
down at the prone wizard.

Hendrek approached the Dealer of Death warily as
the assassin knelt and placed a very large hand
around my master's neck. Both paused, however, to
look my way as I began to flap my elbows and whistle
"The Happy Woodcutter's Song."

Large quantities of haddock appeared some inches
below the hallway's vaulted ceiling. I had not lost
my touch. Haddock, three-day-old dead haddock,
rained on the Dealer, and Hendrek, and Ebenezum,
and myself, and everywhere else the eye could see.
Heemat and Snarks seemed to have disappeared. I
realized I hadn't seen them since our battle with the
Collectors.

I had to act quickly, while the others were still surprised, and before the odor of massive fish death
overcame us all. I slipped and slid my way through a
mountain of scales, over to where I had last seen the
wizard.

The Dealer was no longer there. He had apparently
fled in a vain search for air. But I heard the wizard
groan from somewhere deep within the odiferous
mound. A warclub rose and fell on the other side
of the hallway as Hendrek hacked a passageway

through the amassed fish flesh.

"Quick, Hendrek!" I cried. "Help me get Ebenezum to safety."

Hendrek erupted from the haddock with volcanic force, his enchanted warclub held high.

"Doom!" he cried as I burrowed my way down through the haddock toward the buried Ebenezum. But soon he was at my side, and together we pulled the wizard free of the fish corpses.

"We'll have to get him back to the room," I grunted, taking his feet.

"Nay!" Hendrek replied vehemently. "We should quit this hellish place. That dark assassin is lurking about here somewhere. The sooner we are away from here, the safer." He lifted up Ebenezum's head and shoulders as I might pick up a piece of parchment, quickly and without effort. The warrior turned and led the way through the haddock.

Ebenezum groaned again and opened his eyes. When he spoke at last, his voice was a hoarse whisper.

"The Happy Woodcutter's Song," was all he said.

I nodded. "It's all I could think to do in the circumstances."

The wizard glanced at the floor. "Apparently, your efforts were successful." He snuffled. "It is only at times like this that I am thankful for my malady."

I had been doing my best not to think about the odor, bad enough when I first used the spell in an open field, but quite overpowering in this enclosed space. In fact, I had been doing my best not to breathe at all. If I did not get fresh air in a moment, the fish and I would be much closer.

"Look!" Hendrek cried. "A stairway!" The warrior led us to a dark portico in the wall, which indeed led to a staircase that descended into further darkness.

Ebenezum insisted upon walking. So we set him down between us, keeping the large bulk of Hendrek in the lead. The darkness deepened as we went down, stairs worn smooth by years of use. I was forced to hold on to Ebenezum's robes as he kept a hand against Hendrek's armor-plated back. When at last we reached a landing, the darkness was total.

Hendrek bumped against something wooden and hollow-sounding.

"Doom!" he said.

A door was flung open before us. We were blinded by brilliant torchlight.

"At last!" I heard Heemat's cheerful voice ring in my ears. "Our guests have arrived! Let the entertainment begin!"

THIRTEEN

"Casual amusement can be one of a wizard's greatest problems. After all, when one can conjure virtually anything, what can one do to 'get away from it all'?

"Different wizards arrive at different solutions for their entertainment. A sorcerer of my acquaintance decided to increase his physical prowess through a vigorous program of exercise but found that his new muscles were wont to rip his robes midconjure. Another mage decided to develop the interplay between tongue and teeth so that he could exactly reproduce any insect noise imaginable. He became so successful at this that they discovered his corpse one midsummer's eve, suffocated by six thousand three hundred and two amorous katydids. And of the wizard who tried to start personal communications between humans and sheep . . . well, the less said the better."

—THE TEACHINGS OF EBENEZUM,
Volume XLIV

One of Heemat's many assistants led us to a table deep within this new room. The place seemed very large. Torches had been placed every twenty paces or so around three sides of the room's perimeter, but little light reached the area we now traversed. The room seemed full of people, some hermits, others travelers like ourselves. I had never seen so many people in one place in my entire life. I found it made me almost as nervous as being surrounded by ghosts. My mind caught at a fleeting doubt: Would Vushta be like this? What if I were surrounded by five hundred people upon entering that city of a thousand forbidden delights? Even worse, what if I were surrounded by five hundred women, all young and beautiful, with long red hair cascading across their backs and shoulders, and all of them, every single one, making demands of me?

Well, I would bear it somehow, if only for my master.

"Your table, sirs." Our hooded guide indicated three empty chairs to one side of a small, round table. A chair on the table's far side was occupied. Even in the almost nonexistent illumination, the seated man's size and stature told me at once who he was. We had found the Dealer of Death.

"Doom," Hendrek rumbled.

Heemat bustled over in our direction. "My most honored guests!" he cried, rubbing his stomach happily. "You are among the very privileged few to witness the full, true, and historically accurate saga of Plaugg the Adequately Overwhelming, related through an inspired mesh of dramatic reenactment, dancing, and song! And at the same time and for only a negligible fee, you'll be able to sample the first sacrament of our order. Pastry!'' Heemat patted his stomach for emphasis as another hermit wheeled over a cart laden with cakes, pies, and cookies.

Heemat bowed, then shuffled away. "Make your choices quickly. Soon, you will be entertained!''

My eyes were becoming accustomed to the light, so dim after our confrontation with the torches at the entrance. I could see the Dealer smile. He nodded in my direction.

"I shall be entertained,'' he said.

But before he could speak further, there was a crash of cymbals, and a pair of heavy drapes parted before our table. Seven figures stood before us, all covered completely by monastic robes. Jaunty music began somewhere. The seven figures formed a line and started to kick. From the shapes of their legs I guessed the seven were female. Their singing voices confirmed my supposition:

> *"Seven happy hermits are we,*
> *And we hope you all will see,*
> *You've been brought here by the hand of fate*
> *To hear about Plaugg the Moderately Great!''*

Ebenezum leaned over and tapped the Dealer on the shoulder. "Might we discuss the terms of your contract for a moment?''

The assassin's smile disappeared. "I would rather not. I've become a bit sensitive about the matter. I only neglected one course of study, after all!''

"Indeed,'' the wizard hastily interjected. "I by no means wish to criticize. Actually, should you think on it, a talk might be to your benefit as well. Your vocation is artful death. Consider how much more satisfying a murder might be if it followed a truly satisfying discussion."

The Dealer nodded his head slowly. " 'Tis true a good discussion might help to round my character. I have neglected things for my art."

Ebenezum stroked his beard and smiled. "Indeed. I knew you were a man of reason. I might humbly add that I am a man of some learning, and a discussion with me might help bring out some nuances of thought to aid you in your work."

The Dealer leaned toward the wizard, his gaze intent upon the mage. Ebenezum, for his part, stroked his beard absently, as if lost in deep and sorcerous conjecture. I turned back to the stage. The dancers and singers had vanished, replaced by an old monk who read from a great book:

"And lo, the masses turned unto Plaugg and entreated him to help them in their hour of need. And Plaugg heard them, for his throne was not so great or not so high as to escape the voice of the masses, and was made of second-rate materials besides, studded with elaborate baubles made of adequate cut glass. And Plaugg looked down upon the throng, and speaketh. And lo, he sayeth unto them: 'Not today. I do not feel up to it.' "

"Pray tell," Ebenezum said to the Dealer, "in your current contract, is there a time limit on the delivery of our deaths?"

The Dealer's eyes narrowed. "That is private information. A contract is a sacred . . ." He paused. "Well, perhaps not this contract. No such limit was stipulated."

"Good!" Ebenezum beamed. "We will have time for a really detailed discussion."

The Dealer relaxed. "Yes, perhaps we shall. I have

slighted myself in some areas of study. A few hours of discussion could do no harm.''

"Indeed!" Ebenezum removed his cap and placed it on the table. "Then 'tis time to get down to business. We are very lucky we met, you and I. I am quite skilled in the art of discussion; ask either of my compatriots. We can cover many of the areas neglected in your education. If you'll just give me a day or two to prepare, I'm sure I can devise a truly rewarding course of study. Then, in a few months, only weeks, really, you shall become a fully rounded individual!"

The Dealer stared long and hard at the wizard. A new group of singers and dancers had moved on the platform before us. They were doing a strange dance that seemed to consist of jumping wildly about for a few seconds, then sitting absolutely motionless for minutes at a time. One of the singers, off to the side, exhorted the others to "do the Plaugg." The crowd around us seemed quite taken with the performance.

"Your suggestion has a certain merit," the Dealer murmured, so low as to be almost lost in the crowd noise. "I shall think."

"But you haven't had any pastry!" Heemat had once again appeared tableside, rolling a cart laden with frosted edibles. "You do not want to offend Plaugg, praise his somewhat exalted name!" The hermit heaped pastries before Ebenezum, then moved on to do the same for the glowering Hendrek. "For it has been spoken that Plaugg has a moderately hideous wrath." He quickly ate something small and gooey, then moved on to fill the space before the Dealer. "Of course, no one has ever actually witnessed Plaugg's wrath, praise his fairly magnificent name. But there have been some very strong rumors about what might happen if we were to finally get him mad.''

Heemat moved on to me. "It has been written that in a time of moderate crisis, Plaugg shall return. But what am I saying? You've been watching our dramatic presentation. You probably know more about Plaugg now, praise his reasonable significance, than I do!''

He chuckled to himself about his little joke. I, for one, had absolutely no idea what he was talking about. The performers before us had jumped about and sung a great deal, but there seemed to be no dramatic unity at all to what I'd seen. Of course, my mind had not been entirely on the players. I was somewhat more concerned with the drama that transpired at our small table: the Dealer still lost in thought over my master's proposal; Hendrek munching sullenly at some long, narrow sugar-thing; my master smiling and convivial, casually watching the not-yet-paid assassin's every move.

The Dealer's eyes bored into the layer cake before him. "I have thought," he said after a moment's pause, "and I have decided to accept your offer."

Ebenezum nodded solemnly, no hint on his features that he had just been granted a reprieve from death. I couldn't believe it! The Dealer of Death had accepted the wizard's offer! If my master could talk the Dealer into delaying assassination now, he could surely talk the Dealer out of killing us altogether in a few short days. I vowed never to distrust my master again. I wanted to jump up and down and shout. Still, that would not be businesslike. I filled my mouth with a frosted cupcake instead.

"You are a man of learning, and subtle powers of

speech," the Dealer continued to my master. "You are correct. I must become flexible if I am to improve myself, both within and without my craft."

"Bravo!" my master intoned. "We will immediately begin—"

The Dealer held up his hand for silence. "Unfortunately, you are the only person included in this bargain. Your apprentice and the warrior will, of course, be killed immediately."

My half-eaten cupcake jumped in my throat. I tried to cough and swallow at the same time. Hendrek rose to his feet in a rush, the doomed Headbasher scattering delicacies before it as it skidded across the table. The Dealer yelped in surprise as he was assaulted by a sugar-filled deluge. He managed to dodge all but a single cherry pie.

The assassin wiped sticky red from his eyes. "Two can play at this, warrior," he whispered.

"Doom," Hendrek replied.

"Hendrek, wait!" I cried as I saw the immense man once again raise his warclub. I had had a revelation as the pie hit the Dealer's face. Hendrek could do no better than hold the assassin at bay with his enchanted warclub. But if we were to work together, using the wizard's wits and my beginning spells, we could break through the Dealer's defenses, as the pie, aided by a rain of pastry, had found its mark.

But my master was lost within his robes, hiding from the effects of the enchanted warclub, and Hendrek was full of battle lust and was beyond listening. The warrior dodged a chocolate cake lobbed easily across the table. But the Dealer had only thrown the cake as a decoy, for his right hand held three large, cream-filled éclairs, which shot across the table with deadly force. Yet club was faster than pastry, and I found a large, sodden chocolate mass deflected into my face.

"Gack!" I cried, quite beside myself. Bits of cupcake still lined my throat, and now icing obscured my vision. I expected the hands of the Dealer to descend on me at any moment and tear me into a dozen frosted pieces.

"Blasphemy!" Heemat's voice cut through my panic like a knife dividing a pie into sections. What could happen next? Expectant, I licked the remains of a missile from about my mouth, then wiped away enough cream filling to see.

Heemat stood before a huge crowd, all wearing the same monastic robes. There must have been a hundred hermits gathered there, all staring at the Dealer and myself. Maybe our commotion had interrupted the play.

I was relieved that whatever had occurred, the Dealer had temporarily ceased his attack. However, looking at the grim jaws and cold eyes of the assembled hermits, I had the feeling that what happened next might not be a marked improvement over recent events.

"Blasphemers!" Heemat repeated, his eyes darting back and forth between the Dealer and myself. "In your folly, you have sinned. You have taken what must be eaten, and used it for false purposes. Heathen interlopers, you have profaned the pastry!"

"Profaned the pastry," chanted the crowd of monks behind Heemat.

Heemat shook his head sadly, his eyes looking to the ceiling. "Sometimes I forget." His voice was a hoarse whisper, choked with emotion. "Sometimes my expansive nature gets the better of me. I ask people to be my guests, and share my custom!"

"Share our custom!" the chorus replied.

"And what do you do to thank me for all this?" Heemat waved his arms wildly above his head. "I, who have taken a twenty-year vow of silence, but feel such a compulsion to be friendly to the likes of you that I have managed to fulfill only six weeks of my pledge? Yes, yes, you! We invite you into our homes, give you the very best our humble order has to offer, and you—you—you stamp on the very name of Plaugg the Conservatively Overwhelming!"

"Conservatively Overwhelming," repeated the others.

"Indeed," Ebenezum said, stepping between me and the hermit horde. "I am sure we are all very sorry for departing from established custom among your sect. But we are new here, and perhaps a bit shaky as to the finer points of local tradition. I myself am recovering from a long, severe illness, and must spend much of my time sleeping. The large warrior at my side is possessed by a cursed warclub, and cannot be held responsible for his actions. And what of my apprentice? He is but a youth, and has not yet reached his majority. Surely you cannot blame him for a childish prank or two? We are, all three, quite innocent of malice." He coughed gently into his palm. "As to the gentleman in black . . . well, he will have to speak for himself."

The Dealer's eyes blazed at Ebenezum. "You would so lightly end our agreement, then? Well, my answer is this!" He reached behind him to grab an immense kuchen that covered the entire pastry cart.

The crowd of hermits gasped as one. Apricot filling oozed through the Dealer's fingers.

"No!" Heemat cried. "I will have no more of this!
Take them!"

In an instant, a dozen monks swarmed over the
Dealer. Another instant and the crowd had broken
past Ebenezum. Monks surrounded me. I found
my arms pinioned behind me, the Dealer similarly
trussed at my side. Heemat stood before us both.

"Now listen, blasphemers, and I shall tell you of
Plaugg's judgment, praise his reasonably enormous
name!"

"Reasonably enormous name," the crowd replied.

"We are a strict sect, but we are fair," Heemat
continued. "Before you are put to death, we will give
you a trial, and it is possible that through this trial
you may be redeemed. We have three trials within
our sect. The first is trial by water."

"Trial by water," they all chimed in.

"Unfortunately, being in the middle of the woods,
we are rather lacking in moats, lakes, and other
bodies of water suitable for the task."

"Suitable for the task," the others said.

Heemat rubbed his hands together. "And then, of
course, there's that traditional favorite, trial by
fire."

"Trial by fire," the hermits echoed.

"Unfortunately, we have discovered a side effect
of this trial. Often, the fire gets a bit out of hand, and
we find our hovel burning down as well."

"Burning down as well," the hundred chanted.

"How much better, then, our third form of judgment. And how much truer to the central spirit of the
minor deity that we worship: Plaugg, bless his insubstantial glory!"

"Insubstantial glory!" they parroted.

Heemat leaned so close to me that I could smell his sugar-tainted breath. "Now, interlopers, you shall see the truth. Now, you shall have to face—trial by custard!"

"Trial by custard!" everyone cried.

I was grabbed by two dozen hands and bustled through the curtains onto the stage. My last sight of the room was Ebenezum waving to me. They had not taken him or Hendrek; perhaps, I guessed, because neither of them were covered with pastry.

But Ebenezum was free! That meant he could help me! Didn't it?

I was carried into darkness.

FOURTEEN

"Religion is a personal matter, and those of us in the sorcerous profession would do well to steer clear of it. Still, you will find some situations, say a spell accidentally demolishing someone's holy temple, where you will be given the choice of (one) conversion to their belief, or (two) being sacrificed to their deity. It is only at times like this when one realizes the true depth and beauty of religions, at least until one can find some way out of town."

—THE TEACHINGS OF EBENEZUM,
Volume XXXI

They had bound my hands and feet and left me in the dark. After some time had passed, the door to my cell opened and a lone hermit bearing a candle entered. He silently closed the thick door behind him, then approached the bed on which I lay. He placed the candle on the room's only table, then used both hands to remove his voluminous hood.

It was Snarks.

The hooded demon motioned me to silence. "I should not be here," it whispered, "but somehow I have taken a liking to you. You seem like one of those rare mortals who can be trusted. Perhaps it's your awkward manner and bumbling gait that endears you to me, or the fact that your hair is never properly combed, or the way you misbutton your shirt, or those complexion problems we discussed— but no matter. Whatever it is, you have touched my demon heart. I have decided to help."

I studied Snarks in the dim light. I wasn't sure whether to be grateful or scared out of my mind. Just what came out of a demon heart, anyway?

"Soon," Snarks continued, "the performance will be over in the Great Hall, and it will be time for your trial. Your blasphemy was a lucky break for Heemat, let me tell you. It gives him a much better climax for his evening's entertainment. Before that, all he had planned was another of those big musical numbers. You know: 'Listen to the dancing feet, praising Plaugg the Kind of Neat!' That sort of thing."

I nodded somewhat warily. Thus far, Snarks was not improving my outlook. I wondered if I should call the guards.

"But trial by custard!" the demon exclaimed. "It can be a terrible ordeal if you are unprepared. You and the other blasphemer will each be lowered into one of two vats of custard, each two feet higher than the top of your head. What happens next . . . well, suffocation by custard is a hideous death!"

The demon shivered. "There is only one escape. You must lift your head and eat your way to the surface! I have used my influence to have you dropped into the lemon-filled vat. It is somewhat lighter and less filling than the butterscotch. Once you have a hole to the surface, simply untie your hands and feet, and swim to the doorway at the vat's side. Then you will not only have survived trial by custard, but—''

There was a shuffling noise in the hallway, as if some great weight were being dragged across the cobblestones.

"The other blasphemer is being taken to the Great Hall. I must go. I cannot be seen here!" The demon swallowed hard. "I have no appetite for custard."

Snarks replaced its hood and moved to the door, opening it a crack. The demon looked both ways, turned to me, and waved.

"Grrffmmj!" it called. Then the demon was gone.

Eat my way to the surface? Untie my hands and feet? Snark's words spun through my mind. I had had no idea of the true nature of my ordeal until—

The door to my cell was flung open with such force that it smashed against the wall.

"Now, blasphemer!" Heemat's voice cried, high and full of rage.

And the room began to shake. It was a good quake this time, solid and deep, with a large amount of booming, crashing, and frightened voices in the background. One of the best ones we'd had, actually. I gave it eight out of ten. I wondered absently, tied up on the slab, when I had begun to rate these disturbances.

Heemat picked himself up from the floor when the quakes had finished. He brushed perfunctorily at his robes.

"As I was saying: Now, blasphemer! We will see just what you are made of! Guards, take him away!"

Four burly hermits rushed into the room and lifted me from my pallet. I imagined, in a few short minutes, that I should be made largely of custard.

"Let the trial begin!"

The curtains opened before us. I stood on a high platform, hands and feet tied, a burly hermit guard on either side. A few paces away, the Dealer of Death stood on a similar platform. The ropes around the Dealer appeared somewhat thicker than mine and covered his body in great loops from his chest to his ankles. A dozen burly hermits crowded to either side of him. Between the platforms were two iron vats, each large enough to contain three men. The one closer to me was filled with a quivering bright yellow. The contents of the other were more of a light brown.

The roar of the crowd drew my attention away from the vats. The curtains were open now, revealing an audience that filled the Great Hall.

Was this the room that I had sat in mere moments before? It looked different from my new vantage point, high above the crowd. It was still quite the largest enclosed space I had ever seen, mind you, but from where I stood now, it was definitely just a room, bordered by well-defined, torchlit walls, rather than the limitless vista it had felt like before. And as many people as there were down there, they seemed very small from my platform vantage. For a brief moment, I felt above them, removed.

And then I realized they were all here to see me. Me and the Dealer of Death. We were the attractions here, hundreds of people studying our faces, looking for signs of fear or guilt or even holy reassurance. I knew, somehow, far away, that perhaps I should be afraid. I was, after all, to be dumped into a vat of custard at any moment, and a part of me, deep inside, was screaming in a very tiny voice.

But they had me bound and guarded. There was nowhere to run, no place to hide. And the audience was out there—for me.

They all applauded. It felt wonderful. No more helpmate to the great Ebenezum. I was the center of attention now.

Would it be like this when I was a full-fledged wizard?

I bowed stiffly and lost my balance. Guards grabbed me from the rear, hauling me back from a premature meeting with the custard.

I looked up. The audience was silent. My near accident had caused the assembled masses to gasp as one.

Then, out of the silence came a lone voice, whistling "The Happy Woodcutter's Song."

I looked down to see Ebenezum and Hendrek, seated at the same table the Dealer and I had been spirited away from such a short time ago. Hendrek glowered at the crowd around him and played with the pouch that held the doomed club, Headbasher. Ebenezum shook his head firmly, then pointed to me. I nodded to him, and he touched his whistling mouth.

Did he wish me to whistle as well? Then again, what did I have to lose? If I was about to die in a vat of custard, there were worse ways to go out than whistling.

I began to whistle "The Happy Woodcutter's Song" as well. Ebenezum nodded enthusiastically. So he did want me to whistle!

The wizard had a plan.

Heemat glared at my master, but Ebenezum had

stopped whistling and now seemed content to flap his elbows.

"O Plaugg, who may be among the Great Ones above, or may not, please hear our plea. These two you see before you have blasphemed your name in the midst of our most relatively holy ceremony. So we have brought them to trial before you now, and beseech you to aid us in judging them with your adequate wisdom!"

I noticed that Heemat was staring at me rather fixedly. Perhaps it was because I had whistled. "The Happy Woodcutter's Song" during the entirety of his oration.

Heemat clapped his hands.

"Into the vats!"

Strong arms pushed me into the yellow pool. I barely had time for one quick breath before the sticky mass engulfed me.

I had closed my eyes when my feet hit, but my nose told me I had sunk into the mire. A strong scent of lemon, and then I could no longer breathe at all. I floated for an instant within the thick custard, my hands and feet tied, totally helpless. I fought down a rising panic and tried to remember what Snarks had bade me do. My feet hit the bottom of the vat, and I lifted my head toward the heavens, knowing I must eat now as I had never eaten before.

I opened my mouth, and custard poured in, too much, too fast! I forced my teeth closed, doing my best not to choke, and then, with an effort of will, swallowed. There. That wasn't too bad. Quite tasty, really.

It was just that there was so much more to go.

But I would not panic. I would persevere, for my master, and my future as a wizard, and for Vushta, the city of a thousand forbidden delights. So I ate again, quickly, efficiently, aware that every bite I took might be my last.

For my master! I thought. Ebenezum would be proud of the way I forcefully ate my custard.

For my future! How noble of character a wizard would be if he overcame a challenge like this in his youth. I swallowed a second mouthful, and then a third.

For Vushta! Dear, forbidden Vushta. Surviving an ordeal like this would only make me more prepared for that great city where a single glance might mark a man for life. I opened my mouth wide and let the custard pour.

My teeth closed on air. Air! I swallowed quickly and began to breathe. Air! Sweeter than all the lemon custard in the world! I laughed and began to whistle "The Happy Woodcutter's Song."

But something covered my mouth again. Had the custard shifted? My panic returned. I opened my eyes to see insect feelers waving above my nose.

It was a butterfly.

There was a crash as the vat, burdened with me, hundreds of gallons of custard, and thousands, perhaps millions, of butterflies, could no longer support the weight. I found myself floating off the stage on a river of custard.

Snarks called from the platform overhead:

"He has survived the trial by custard!"

"But—" Heemat began, rather flustered. "He can't—" He rubbed his bald head and smiled. "I suppose he can."

Hendrek waded into the yellow torrent and grabbed me before I could be swept beyond the wizard's table. He placed me on a seat above the now dwindling custard tide. Ebenezum, of course, was still sneezing.

When my master composed himself, I thanked him for not using the haddock spell.

Ebenezum nodded happily. "Butterflies were all that was needed. And it was better that I saved you without alienating our hosts. Undo Wuntvor's bonds, would you, Hendrek?"

The large warrior did as he was asked. In the meantime, Ebenezum went on to explain what a great thing it was that we had accomplished—collaborative magic. I had whistled, he had flapped and wriggled, and the magic had still occurred. That was important, since in flapping and wriggling, he wasn't doing anything sorcerous. Thus, the magical implications did not affect his malady until the spell was already successfully completed, whereas if he had tried to accomplish the entire spell himself, he would have collapsed in a sneezing fit halfway through the song.

"So you see what this means?" Ebenezum concluded. "Whole vistas of magic are open to me again. Together, Wuntvor, we might even find a cure!"

A cure? This was all too much. First, almost drowning in a vat of custard, and now this! I pictured myself fated to return to Wizard's Woods without the slightest chance of seeing Vushta for years to come.

Ebenezum was much too excited to notice my mood. "And it was never so important as now to muster our magical resources. While you were preparing for your ordeal, I have had discussions with Hendrek. His demonic tormentors were able to locate him much too quickly after our escape from Urfoo."

"Doom," Hendrek added.

"Which fits the pattern we began to see on our journey to Vushta. Wuntvor, there are far too many demons loose in the world. Something new is coming from the Netherhells. And now, Wuntvor, that certain inconveniences are out of the way"—he nodded to the stage and the still-upright vat of butterscotch custard—"we can find out just what that something is."

In my relief at being alive, I had quite forgotten what was still transpiring on the stage. By now, the live butterflies had all flown out among the audience, and they had swept the dead butterflies, custard, and broken bits of vat away.

Heemat stood, arms outstretched, on one of the platforms. His eyes surveyed the audience. He cleared his throat.

The remaining vat tipped over sideways, and the Dealer of Death tumbled out. The vat rolled about so that its innards faced the audience. There was no custard left in there at all. The iron sides had been licked clean.

The Dealer burped.

"Certain inconveniences appear to have returned," Ebenezum remarked. He tugged at his beard thoughtfully. "But perhaps it will take him a few minutes to digest. We must talk to Snarks, and quickly. He has knowledge of the Netherhells that is important to our guest and, yes, may be important to our very lives."

The Dealer groaned and tried to stand. His stomach appeared somewhat larger than it had before. Heemat ran back and forth across the upper platform, his hands rubbing together so fast that I expected to see sparks.

"Two have passed!" he cried. "Two! Two! Never in the history of the worship of Plaugg, bless his mundane magnificence, have two survived the trial! We must—we must— It is time for a conference!"

A heavily cowled figure scooted past our table. Hendrek grabbed his hood as Ebenezum held his wizardly nose. The doomed warrior had been correct in his assumption. It was Snarks.

"Good Snarks!" Ebenezum managed, doing his best not to sneeze. "We must speak—we must— spee—sp—" He quickly grabbed his cap and sneezed therein. "Pardon. Something is happening with the Nether—with the Ne— Ne— N—" Three sneezes this time, in rapid succession. Ebenezum held his cap at arm's length with some distaste. "Snarks, you mu— mus— Drat! Wuntvor! 'Tis up to you!"

The wizard fell beneath the table, lost in a sneezing fit.

"Indeed," I began. What should I ask this all-too-honest demon? I wanted to make my master proud! But there wasn't much time. Already the Dealer of Death was leaping about the stage, involved in a complex series of calisthenics designed, I was sure, to aid digestion and free custard-stiffened muscles.

"Indeed," I said again. "I believe you come from the Netherhells?"

"No, no, no," Snarks replied. "Actually, you know for a fact that I come from the Netherhells. You should think more before you speak, you know. Inexact language, inappropriate questions. Sometimes I don't know how you humans make it from day to day."

"Snarks!" I cried, a bit more loudly than perhaps I should. I would not be upset by his demon tongue.

"We have reason to believe there's a plot afoot in the Netherhells!"

"And good reason it is, too," Snarks replied. "There are always plots afoot in the Netherhells. It's part of the charm of the place. But I imagine, in your bumbling way, you're asking me if there's one particular plot, a large, dangerous plot, perhaps, that could threaten all of humankind. Is that what you want to ask of me?"

I nodded my head. Perhaps it was best not to speak at all and just let the demon talk.

"Well, the answer is yes. Now, if you'll excuse me, I'm late for the conference."

"Doom!" Hendrek remarked as Snarks leapt up onstage. Ebenezum blew his nose.

Heemat had already turned away from the huddled monks and once again began to address the audience.

"Ladies and gentlemen, fellow believers, and our guests. Never in the history of Plauggdom has such a modestly blessed event as this occurred. Two in our midst have been tested, and found reasonably worthy. Even Plaugg himself, bless his marginal magnificence, must be looking down from his moderate height and—"

A small gray storm cloud appeared over Heemat's head, the kind that meant a moment's rain before it disappeared. Heemat paused midsentence to gape as the cloud took on the shape of a man, wearing rumpled gray robes and a distracted expression. The disheveled floating man squinted out into the audience.

"Pardon me," he muttered in a timorous voice. "I'm not so sure I should be here."

Heemat, his fellows on the stage, and all the

hermit-monks in the audience had fallen to their knees. The assemblage looked to the rumpled man overhead and spoke with one voice.

"Plaugg!"

FIFTEEN

"So you think you know great, nail-biting excitement, you think you know truly abject fear, you think you know total and complete despair, you think you know the incredibly degenerate underside of this world we live in, and the ridiculously despicable lengths that your fellow man can sink to, more rotten, more putrid than the lowest form of fungus. . . . Oh. You are a sorcerer as well. Then perhaps you do."

—FURTHER CONVERSATIONS WITH EBENEZUM,
Volume III

"Oh, maybe I'm a little early," Plaugg said, seemingly to himself. "Yes, of course, that must be it. I'm early!"

Ebenezum watched the minor deity with some trepidation. Once again, the wizard held his nose.

"Oh, come now, come now," Plaugg said, singling the wizard out. "I won't let you sneeze around me. It's the least I can do."

The wizard looked up at the gray, rumpled deity. He breathed in and out without ill effect. "Do you mean to say," the wizard said cautiously, "that you have the power to cure my affliction?"

"Well, that's a problem, isn't it?" Plaugg clasped his hands together. "Not exactly, no. We minor deities can only do so much, you know. Unfortunately, I can only cure your affliction with regard to myself."

"Oh." Ebenezum frowned. "Pity."

"Yes, isn't it," Plaugg agreed. "It's one of the problems with being a minor deity. You only get so much power, and oh, the responsibility that comes with it! You could hardly imagine. Always having to please the faithful. After all, what do you imagine I'm doing here now? Although come to think of it, that hasn't happened yet, has it?"

"O reasonably beneficent Plaugg!" Heemat cried from the platform.

"Yes, yes, I'll be with you in a moment," the minor deity remarked. "As soon as I finish talking with this gentleman here. You wouldn't believe how long it's been since I've had a good talk. It's one of the problems with my profession, I'm afraid. You get a lot of worship in my position, but very little good conversation."

Ebenezum nodded. "What would you like to talk about? You wouldn't want to tell us why you're here?"

"Oh, that." Plaugg sighed. "Duty. I do sometimes get tired of all that. Being a minor deity is really more trouble than it's worth. Your worshipers never look you in the eye, and should you even attempt to speak to them, they start sacrificing things to you. Sacrifices and more sacrifices, at the drop of a hat.

Now I ask you, what use have I got for a dead goat?''

"Plaugg, do you demand a sacrifice?" Heemat
queried.

"See what I mean?" The deity frowned. "Oh.
Don't get me wrong. Heemat and his group are a
perfectly nice bunch of worshipers. There are just
certain problems with being a minor deity. For one
thing, there's very little chance for promotion. And
the hours! I've been thinking seriously about getting
into another line of work.''

"What do you wish from us, Adequate One?"
Heemat continued.

"Mostly that you stop asking questions," the deity
replied. "Believe it or not, I am here for a reason.''

There was silence in the Great Hall. All was still.
I noticed that sometime after the appearance of
Plaugg, the Dealer of Death had managed to quit the
stage. I decided to search the room for him, but I
didn't have to look far. He stood just behind
Ebenezum. He smiled at me.

"Oh," Plaugg said as the silence lengthened. "I
suppose you want to know why I'm here. Well, that's
a reasonable request, and you are my worshipers,
after all. Very well. I am here to band us together
through the coming crisis.''

The coming crisis? I did not like the sound of that.
Hendrek muttered darkly at my side.

A hermit directly below the deity pulled back his
hood. It was Snarks.

"You mean the attack from the Netherhells?''

"Why, yes, didn't I say that?" Plaugg rubbed at
his balding pate as he stared in the distance. "Oh. I
suppose I didn't." He looked down at the ground
beneath our feet. "Here it comes now.''

It started more as a feeling than a sound. Deep, far

deeper than any of the quakes we heard before, as if it started at the center of the world.

"Now I want us all to be ready!" Plaugg cried, his voice much stronger than before. "In a few minutes, we're going to see all kinds of demons! But they've never dealt with anyone like Plaugg's hermits before!"

The noise grew beneath our feet.

"Doom," Hendrek intoned. He unsheathed the doomed club, Headbasher. Ebenezum backed away to a safer distance.

"Now I want every one of you to do your utmost!" the deity encouraged. "Drive those demons back where they came from. Do it for Plaugg!"

The rumbling had become a vibration in the floor. It was difficult to remain standing. The Dealer walked up to me.

"It appears I must once again postpone your deaths," he said behind his childlike smile. "Oh, well. This is the most fun I've ever had, ever!" He flexed his muscles and stared expectantly at the floor.

I was glad someone was having a good time. The quake was quite loud by now. Plaugg had to shout to be heard.

"Okay." He pointed a quivering finger at the middle of the audience. "I imagine the Netherhells will break through just about there. And I'm pretty good at guessing these things, let me tell you. Comes with the job, I suppose. So everyone should spread out to the corners of the room. And pile those tables up in front of you, why don't you? It'll protect you from some of the molten debris."

"What, are some of you leaving?" Plaugg shook his balding head. "Now, you don't want to get me angry, do you? My wrath may not be in the big leagues, but it *is* moderately great, let me tell you! Oh, weapons? You need weapons? Well, all right, then. I do sometimes get carried away with myself. You'll have to excuse me."

I looked to my master, and he turned away from the deity, a bemused smile on his face.

"We find ourselves in the middle again, Wuntvor," remarked the mage. He held his nose as Hendrek approached.

"Doom," the large warrior intoned. "We shall be overwhelmed by those things!" He shifted the great warclub nervously from hand to hand.

This whole situation seemed to have gotten totally out of control. "Perhaps we should relocate," I suggested delicately.

Ebenezum shook his head. "I fear we should have to relocate to another world entirely. I think that for the first time in our travels, we have stumbled on something that is truly serious."

I swallowed hard. My hands ached for my stout oak staff. This was serious? Then what were all our battles and narrow escapes of the past few weeks? For a brief moment, I even longed for the utter peace and boredom of our home in the Western Kingdoms.

"Okay, now, they're almost here!" Plaugg shrieked at the top of his lungs. The rumbling had redoubled again. I tried to speak to my master, but I couldn't even hear myself. "Is everybody ready? I know you can do it! Just do what you do best!"

The deity paused to look at Ebenezum and myself. "Now, I will ask you folks not to do the fish trick. I know it has worked before, but this situation is different. And I simply refuse to work around large quantities of dead haddock. I'm sorry, but we all have our limits.

"Here they come! Here they come!" Plaugg was beginning to sound really excited. "Let's hear the call and defeat them all! *Do it for Plaugg!*"

That's when the earth really began to shake. I was thrown off my feet and bounced across the room. I tried to follow Plaugg's advice and crawl toward the wall.

And then the ground was ripped in two. I grabbed onto a table just to hold on to something solid. The table shifted and dragged me along with it toward the crack that widened in the floor. I was sliding straight for a pit that dropped all the way down to the Netherhells! I could hear the death screams of those who fell before me; screams that started loud and shrill, then faded with distance. I tried to find something else to grab onto, but everything was slipping away with me.

And then it stopped, as suddenly as it had begun. I found myself face to face with a troll.

"Slobber!" the troll remarked.

I hit the troll with the table. The table broke.

"Slobber!" the troll repeated.

"Oh, if my teachers could only see me now!" A large hand appeared before me and plucked the troll off the ground. An incredibly cheerful Dealer of Death stood at my side.

"This is the first chance I've had to strangle a troll," the Dealer enthused.

"No slob—" was all the troll had time to say.

A great, deep voice spoke somewhere behind me:

"Come on, my minions!
  Grab all of them!

And tear every one of them
Limb from limb!"

Dust filled the air. It was impossible to see more than a few feet. Still, I had a cold feeling in my stomach about that voice. Ony one poet could be that bad.

"Roar for the Netherhells
Let your colors unfurl,
In a matter of hours
We will rule this world!"

Dimly, I could see a great blue form standing above the rubble. Yes, it was the demon Guxx.

"We'll rule this world
With pride and pomp,
And so for the moment
Let's Stomp! Stomp! Stomp!"

This was terrible! There were demons everywhere! Every second the dust cleared, there seemed to be more of them, as if they sprang from the dust itself. If someone didn't do something quickly, we were all going to die. Worse yet, the last sounds to assail our ears would be Guxx's doggerel verse.

But then a higher voice cried out from across the room:

"Give me a P!"

A few ragged "P"'s were shouted here and there.

"Give me an L!"

I cried, "L!" with the others. The response was stronger now.

"Quickly now!" Guxx screamed back at us.

"Don't let them rally! We need a death count we can tally!"

But the other voice would not be silenced.

"Give me an A!"

The dust had settled enough now so that I could see halfway around the room. A small red demon jumped for my throat. I still held a table leg, all that remained of the weapon I had used on the troll. I batted the small demon high in the air.

"A!" I cried.

Hendrek was at my side. His warclub wove a fantastic pattern in the air, knocking the senses from a dozen demons in as many seconds. Cries of "What?" "Who am I?" and "What am I doing here?" could be heard from those demons who were still conscious, evidence of Headbasher's hellish powers.

"U!" Hendrek cried with the rest of us.

I looked about for my master.

"Give me a G!"

The Dealer of Death stood at my other side, moving so fast that he made Hendrek's attack look like a Sunday stroll. Demon arms and legs were all around him. Sometimes they had demons attached.

"G!" the Dealer cried with the others. He laughed and began to whistle.

I spotted Heemat and Snarks as part of a circle of about a dozen hermits. Each of them held a stick a bit thicker and a little shorter than my usual stout oak walking staff. They were using them quite effectively to hold off a horde of demons and doing occasional greater damage among the fiends as well.

"Give me another G!"

"Another G!" they cried together joyously.

And then I saw my master. He had backed up

against a pile of rubble, holding his nose with both hands.

A particularly large and hairy troll advanced upon him.

"Slobber," the troll said in its gravel voice.

"And what does that spell?" came the voice from on high.

Ebenezum's face had become an odd shade of purplish red. His head reared back involuntarily. He could no longer hold his malady within.

The troll felt the full force of the nasal blow. The muscular creature jumped and screamed, shaking mucus from its legs and arms.

"No slobber! No slobber!" it cried as it ran back to the pit that led to the Netherhells.

"Plaugg!" a hundred voices joined together to shout.

"What's that spell?" the first voice prompted again.

"Plaugg!" We all joined in this time, a thousand voices strong.

"One more time!" The voice sounded delirious with joy.

I saw Ebenezum take a deep breath and join in.

"Plaugg!"

The world froze around us. Or, more specifically, the demons froze, in whatever position they had assumed when we had let loose with our final cheer. What dust remained in the air had vanished as well. Our surroundings were as cool and clear as a spring morning.

Plaugg hung where we'd left him in the middle of the air.

"There," he said. "That's much better, isn't it?"

Guxx screamed in rage from atop a large pile of

dead hermits. Apparently he was the only demon unaffected by our chanted magic.

"You think to stop Guxx and his demons,
  But I will find a way to free them!"

Ebenezum blew his nose. "Beware!" he called to Plaugg. "His power grows with every rhyme!"

"Even that one?" The deity shook his head in disbelief. "But who am I to judge? I don't make the rules. Or at least not many of them."

The large blue demon flexed its muscular arms. Its claws had grown back since its fight with Ebenezum.

"You try to stop Guxx with your jokes,
  But I will live to see you choke!"

I saw the demons nearest me twitch slightly. Guxx's poetry would bring them back to life!

"My, you are a serious fellow, aren't you?" Plaugg replied. "Just a second, now, and I'll nicely send you back where you came from."

Ebenezum began to sneeze again. The demon's magic was returning!

Guxx bared its razor fangs.

"You'll not have a moment!
  You'll have no time at all,
  For me and my demons
  Will cause your downfall!"

All the demons nearby definitely quivered.

"Oh, this fellow can be tiresome, can't he?" Plaugg replied. "Give me a moment, won't you? I hardly ever do these physical manifestations, and usually they only allow me to show up as burning moss. I'm not high enough up on the ladder to do bushes, you know. But do I mind?''

Guxx leapt up and raked the air with its claws. You could tell the demon was feeling better with every passing moment.

"You've had your chance,
  You heavenly fool,
  But now 'tis time
  For demons to rule!''

I saw the demon closest to me blink repeatedly.

"Name calling, is it, then?" Plaugg retorted. "It's no longer a gentleman's game, I see. If I wasn't having so much trouble figuring out just how to make things work in this form, you wouldn't even have time to carry on this way. Perhaps I should have shown up as the burning tree moss after all. It's not very intellectually stimulating, though, let me tell you.''

"I've had enough of your lies and talk!
  Fellow demons, arise, to work!''

The frozen demons didn't move.

"Ahem," Guxx remarked. "Not good enough, huh? Well, let's try this:

"Come on demons, arise, dig in,
  For we have a world to win!''

A few of the demons yawned and stretched.

"O reasonably mighty Plaugg!" Heemat cried. "Do something. Please?''

"I'm sorry," the deity replied. "I can't be rushed. Oh, wait a second. Is this it?" He shook his posterior three times. Nothing happened.

"Arise demons! Come now, make haste!
For we have a world to waste!"

The demons awoke en masse.

"Quick! Do something!" Heemat screamed. "Er . . . we beseech you! Please!"

"Yes, yes, I'll have it soon." Plaugg bit his lower lip. "You'll just have to handle them for a moment or two."

"This one is mine!" the Dealer of Death called, launching himself toward Guxx. "I always wanted to strangle a *really* big demon!"

Guxx struck out at the approaching assassin, but the Dealer was too fast. Guxx held nothing but itself in its claws, and the Dealer held the demon in a stranglehold from behind.

"Demons, demons, to work, to work!
We must overwhelm these pitiful—urracht!"

The Dealer tightened his hold.

"Wait a second!" Plaugg cried as the demons once again began to rend and tear. "I have it!" He shook his posterior three times and snapped his fingers.

Trumpets sounded from on high. I heard the flutter of wings above us, too, as if the air were filled with invisible birds. An even larger hole appeared in the middle of the room. The denizens of the Netherhells shrieked as one as they were pulled back to their home.

When the hole had closed, Heemat and ten other

hermits rose from where they sat on Snarks.

"Can't risk losing a convert." Heemat smiled.

"Vsspllthmm Quxx!" Snarks replied.

"There's one left?" Plaugg frowned. "But I quite specifically remember getting an exact count."

It was then that I realized the Dealer was no longer among us.

"Well," Plaugg said. "It's been nice. Don't call me, I'll call you. I need a vacation. It's a problem with my position, you know. Do you think they give me any time off at all?"

And with that, Plaugg was gone as well.

Ebenezum blew his nose.

"Now our real work begins."

SIXTEEN

"Beginnings and endings are, for the most part, artificial constructs. You say you begin when you are born, but what of those months spent growing in the womb? Endings are hazier still, for further things may occur that extend and enlarge the earlier story. And that is my final sentence on the subject. Or perhaps this one is the final sentence. No, most assuredly what I write now is the final word on the matter. But now that I think upon it, perhaps this—"

—THE TEACHINGS OF EBENEZUM, Volume LVII
(Abridged)

"What do you mean, you won't pay?"

Ebenezum stared evenly at a scarlet Heemat.

"As you recall, good Heemat, we paid for basic room and board on arrival. At that point, you gave us no indication of the extent of additional charges we might entail."

"But surely you must realize that a hovel of our standing—"

The wizard glanced through the three sheets of parchment, each one filled with a list of charges written in a tiny hand. "Now, I see you list a broken table among the charges. That, at least, is a reasonable request. I suggest that you contact the man who broke said table. He is, I believe, currently residing in the Netherhells." He slapped the bill before him. "Ninety-six gallons of lemon custard? You would dare charge us—" Ebenezum became speechless with wizardly rage.

Heemat shrugged. "Someone has to pay it."

"Indeed." The wizard spoke all too evenly. I had seen my master like this before. I stood as far back as I could possibly get.

"I will say the following only once," the wizard remarked. "Sir, how would you feel if you were turned into a frog?"

"A frog," Heemat repeated. He looked down at his feet. Perhaps he imagined them webbed. He looked back at Ebenezum, in full sorcerous regalia.

"A frog," he said again. He snatched the bills from Ebenezum's grasp. "Well, perhaps there are a few mistakes herein. Occasionally, our accountants do become overzealous. I shall review the account personally."

"Please do so." The wizard's voice had grown considerably calmer. "We will, of course, be taking Snarks with us as well."

"You're taking Snarks?" The color returned to Heemat's face. "You cheat me of my rightful monies, and then you demand my best assistant? I'll have you know—"

"I understand the lily pads are very nice this time of year," Ebenezum interjected.

"Lily pads." Heemat went white. "Too long have

I neglected my vow of silence. It is high time I reinstituted my most holy pledge, this very instant." Heemat clamped his lips together tight.

"I have always admired holy men," Ebenezum replied as Hendrek joined us. The large warrior had Snarks in tow.

The demon hermit removed its cowl. "They are right, friend Heemat," it said. "I saw what was going on before I was expelled from the Netherhells. There are certain demons down there who are tired of being constantly under the earth. They would like to see what it feels like to control the surface as well. And these factions are finding greater demonic favor every day."

"Far too true," Ebenezum agreed from a safe distance. "My 'prentice and I have seen a massive overabundance of sorcerous activity in our travels to fabled Vushta, and I have long feared consequences such as these. So the four of us, Wuntvor, myself, Snarks, and the warrior Hendrek, must continue to Vushta in all haste. At first, I wished to visit this city for personal reasons. Now, though, I must make preparations to warn the great Wizard's University, and help them prepare for the tremendous sorcerous battle that is to come."

Heemat nodded silently.

"So you actually will keep to your vow of silence," Snarks remarked. "It will make up for all the times you talked too much. And you know, friend Heemat, you, too, could stand to lose a few pounds. And of course, I would be remiss if I did not mention grrllp xxzzttff krll."

Hendrek had replaced the cowl on the demon's head.

"Doom," the warrior remarked.

Heemat, who seemed on the edge of saying something, glanced at the wizard and did not.

"We appreciate your reasonableness in this matter," Ebenezum continued to the hermit. "And due to the severity of the matter, we have taken the liberty of borrowing a horse and cart from your stables. Oh, have no fear! They'll only be gone for a few months at most! That is, so long as we're not attacked by demons. Still, I want you to know that all four of us appreciate your sacrifice, so that we may get some much needed rest on our way to Vushta."

He pointed to the kitchen. "Wuntvor, go and fetch those two sacks of provisions I had put aside."

I did as I was told, doing my best to ignore Heemat, who had once again turned the red of a truly spectacular sunset.

And so we were on our way once again to Vushta, city of a thousand forbidden delights that could truly mark a man for life. I couldn't remember the last time I was in such a good mood. A light rain fell as the cart made its way through the woods, as refreshing a cold, light rain as I had ever felt. I hummed to myself as I urged the horse forward. Coming from a farming background, I had as much experience as anyone with animals.

Ebenezum sat on the seat next to me on the cart. It was plain that the wizard was still exhausted. Every minute or two he began to nod, until the bumps of the cart jarred him awake. Hendrek sat directly behind us, glowering as usual. Snarks sat even farther back in the cart, under the canvas covering, doing whatever Snarks did deep within those robes.

A bloodcurdling scream came from the bushes. A man dressed only in a loincloth rushed toward the cart, dagger held before him. His bare foot hit a rock as he ran up the road. He tripped. Somehow, he managed to impale himself on his own weapon.

"Another assassin," I remarked absently as we rode by the corpse.

"Indeed," Ebenezum replied. "It's all rather comforting, isn't it?"

And indeed it was. Ebenezum finally fell to sleep in earnest, and I continued to drive the cart, to Vushta and destiny.

Oh, what a wonderful world!

Headline books are available at your bookshop or newsagent, or can be ordered from the following address:

Headline Book Publishing PLC
Cash Sales Department
PO Box 11
Falmouth
Cornwall
TR10 9EN
England

UK customers please send cheque or postal order (no currency), allowing 60p for postage and packing for the first book, plus 25p for the second book and 15p for each additional book ordered up to a maximum charge of £1.90 in UK.

BFPO customers please allow 60p for postage and packing for the first book, plus 25p for the second book and 15p per copy for the next seven books, thereafter 9p per book.

Overseas and Eire customers please allow £1.25 for postage and packing for the first book, plus 75p for the second book and 28p for each subsequent book.